Longarm's .45 was quic
gauge. Longarm ripped off two quick shots. The first hit roughly in the middle of the flour sack and snapped the fellow's head back. The second took him low in the side and spun him around before he collapsed like a marionette with its strings cut.

The robber hit the floor hard and did not even bounce. His shotgun, fortunately, clattered down without discharging.

The second fellow, possibly smarter than the first, did not waste time attempting to shoot Longarm. Instead, he jumped forward toward the people he had come there to rob.

He jammed the muzzle of his shotgun against Samantha Morris's back and shoved her out into the room without so much as glancing down at his dying partner.

But then perhaps he had seen enough of that already.

"Nobody move. Nobody. That means you, cowboy. I'll blow this little lady in two if you try anything. Believe it."

TABOR EVANS

LONGARM

AND THE
LYING LADIES

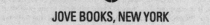

JOVE BOOKS, NEW YORK

THE BERKLEY PUBLISHING GROUP
Published by the Penguin Group
Penguin Group (USA) LLC
375 Hudson Street, New York, New York 10014

USA • Canada • UK • Ireland • Australia • New Zealand • India • South Africa • China

penguin.com

A Penguin Random House Company

LONGARM AND THE LYING LADIES

A Jove Book / published by arrangement with the author

For information, address: The Berkley Publishing Group,
a division of Penguin Group (USA) LLC,
375 Hudson Street, New York, New York 10014.

ISBN: 978-0-515-15379-8

PUBLISHING HISTORY
Jove mass-market edition / November 2013

PRINTED IN THE UNITED STATES OF AMERICA

10 9 8 7 6 5 4 3 2 1

Cover illustration by Milo Sinovcic.

Chapter 1

Custis Long woke slowly, luxuriating in the feel of the satin coverlet drawn up beneath his chin and the warmth of the perfumed body that lay snug against his side.

He yawned. Must have fallen asleep for a little while. Well, no wonder after the ride the girl . . . What the hell was her name? Ah. Victoria. That was it. Oh, she had given him one wild ride, that was for sure. He wondered if he should wake her for another tussle of the beast with two backs or if he should just slip out and go home for a little sleep before he had to get up again.

He had to be at the office on time in the morning. Henry said there was something special going on that the boss wanted him in on and that he should not be late. For a change.

The deputy United States marshal known as Longarm yawned again. He could hear Victoria's breathing slow and steady beside him. She was quite a girl, Victoria was. Small and soft and cuddly. Wild as a march hare in bed, though.

Thinking about Victoria and about her particular desires, Longarm felt the beginnings of an erection. The last thing he remembered, he had been fairly sure he was so tuckered out and thoroughly sated that he would not be able to get a hard-on for the next week. Now here he was just minutes later and already rising again.

The question was whether he should wake Victoria or just quietly dress and go home.

Where had he tossed his clothes, anyway? It was a good thing there was enough light in the room that he could see to find his clothes without lighting a lamp, and . . . Why was there so much light in the room?

Hadn't he blown the lamp out a little while ago?

Wasn't it . . . Oh, Lord. There was sunlight streaming in past the edges of the heavy drapes the woman used to keep out the light so she could sleep late after performing in the final scenes of her play.

That meant it was past daybreak. That meant he must have fallen hard asleep and spent the entire night with her.

Lordy!

Longarm threw the covers aside, never mind if he woke Victoria, and leaped out of bed. He grabbed his clothing off the chair by her makeup table and was still dressing when he hit the door practically at a dead run.

His vest was still unbuttoned and his string tie in a coat pocket when he got to the street and looked frantically around for a hansom cab.

He saw one. Waved for the driver's attention. When the hansom reached him, Longarm climbed in practically before he could shout, "Federal Building. And I am in one helluva hurry, mister."

The driver laughed. But then perhaps he was accustomed to seeing disheveled men dash out of this entertainment district hotel.

The man snapped his whip over the ears of his horse, and the cab lurched forward and settled into a brisk trot through Denver's early morning traffic.

By the time the hansom came to a stop in front of the stone steps facing Colfax Avenue, Longarm was tucked and tidied and fully dressed from his brown Stetson hat down to his calf-high black cavalry boots.

Longarm stepped down onto the red brick street, fished a coin out of his pocket, and handed it to the driver. "Thanks, friend."

He took the steps two at a time and raced inside to U.S. Marshal William Vail's first floor office.

"You're late again," Billy Vail's clerk, Henry, said as Longarm skidded inside.

"Has he called for me yet?" Longarm asked as he hung his Stetson on the hat rack in the outer office.

"No. You're lucky," Henry said with a grin, adding, "again."

"I got, uh, caught in traffic," Longarm said.

"I believe you too," Henry told him. "But before you go in to see the boss, I'd suggest you wipe some of that lipstick off your face." His grin became wider. "Unless you've started wearing makeup."

"Oh, shit," Longarm mumbled as he reached for a handkerchief he could use to scrub his face with.

"Henry," Billy Vail called from within his private office. "Is Deputy Long out there?"

"Right here, Boss," Longarm called back to him, frantically wiping his face.

He was still stuffing the handkerchief back into his pocket when he adopted a casual air and sauntered into the boss's office to see what this morning call was all about.

Chapter 2

"Long, you look like hell," Billy Vail said. He was standing behind his desk and as usual appeared fresh, although he had probably been at work for several hours already.

"Thank you, Boss. And ain't that a helluva greeting," Longarm said.

"Well, you could at least shave before you come in, and that shirt looks like it could use a trip to the laundry," Vail replied. "What did you do? Sleep in it last night?"

"There's a explanation, Boss, but I don't think you want to hear it." Longarm took a seat without waiting to be asked.

"No, you're probably right about that," Vail agreed. He turned his swivel chair around and sat in it, then turned it to face Longarm.

"Mind if I smoke?" Longarm asked.

"Go ahead if you like."

"First smoke o' the morning always tastes fine."

"First?" Vail said.

Longarm shrugged. He did not really want to tell Billy where he had been until mere minutes ago. He pulled out a cheroot and bit the twist off, then slipped the scrap of tobacco into his coat pocket rather than toss it onto the floor. Billy could be picky about such things. He took out a match and flicked it alight with his thumbnail, then lit the slender cigar.

"Anyway," Billy said, leaning forward over his desk, "the reason I wanted to see you this morning was to give you an, um, an assignment. Not an entirely ordinary one, however. I don't want you to necessarily make any arrests. Basically I want . . . the attorney general wants . . . you to look into the, um, into the possibility that someone in the New Mexico Territory . . . that, um, that there may be, well, irregularities in that district."

"Boss," Longarm said, "what the hell are you talkin' about? Why don't you quit dancing around the edges o' the thing an' tell me straight-out what the problem is."

Vail paused to take a deep breath and start over. "You're right. All right then, here it is. The attorney general thinks one of our people down there, perhaps more than one, has been, um, subverted, you might say."

"He thinks someone is dirty?" Longarm asked.

"In a nutshell . . . yes."

"Who?"

Billy swiveled his chair around to face the window, sat silently for a moment, and then turned back around to face Longarm. "Deputy Ricardo Gomez. He operates in the south of the territory, lives in a town called Salt Springs. The man works for Marshal Ben Phillips. You've met Ben, I believe."

Longarm nodded. "Nice fella as I recall."

"Yes, he is. They say Gomez is too. The man finds a good many fugitives trying to pass through his territory. Grabs them up and transports them to Santa Fe and turns them over to Phillips. He collects fees on the prisoners and makes a nice piece of change from his transportation mileage too. Has his own prison wagon to haul them in, I understand."

"He must be busy to justify that," Longarm said.

"Like I said, he grabs them when they try to pass through."

"Fine," Longarm said. "So what is the problem?"

Again Billy hesitated before he spoke. "There is one gang, Longarm, that Gomez cannot seem to find. Fugitives all and bad ones at that, but they seem to slip through his grasp like so many grains of sand."

"And you think he might be in cahoots with them?" Longarm guessed.

Billy reluctantly nodded. "It seems . . . possible."

"And Marshal Phillips?"

Billy sighed. "Probably not, but . . ."

"But if Gomez is bent, Phillips might be too?"

"I can't rule out the possibility," Billy said. "The attorney general asked me to send a man down there incognito to look the situation over and report back about it. Not necessarily to make an arrest but to . . . find out."

"And that man would be me," Longarm said.

"Exactly. The attorney general has authorized funds to provide a cover story. Something you would find comfortable." Billy smiled for the first time since Longarm entered his office. "*Not*, I emphasize, not as a whiskey salesman, however."

"Aw, shit, Billy, that woulda been my first choice."

"And not as a wandering gambler either. I've seen you play cards, and I fear the entire United States Treasury Department would not be able to afford to cover your losses if you were to go down there as a gambler."

"What then?"

"Pick something you would be comfortable with."

"A doctor specializing in female complaints?" Longarm suggested.

"I'm beginning to think I should send someone else," Billy said.

"Don't worry, Boss. I'll think o' something. When do you want me to go?"

"Take the morning train tomorrow. That will give Henry time to make a few arrangements. You will need cash since you won't be able to use government vouchers this time, and you will need a way to contact us if you have questions or need more money. Go home now and do whatever packing you need, then come back here after lunch. Henry will have some cash ready and instructions about a fake address you can wire if need be."

Longarm nodded and tapped the ash off the glowing tip of his cheroot. "Can do, Boss."

"I . . . we . . . are hoping that you will find no irregularities down there, Custis. But it is something we have to know. We can't allow justice to be subverted. Not by anyone and not for anything."

"Yes, sir. I do understand that." He stood and paused for a moment in front of the marshal's broad desk, then turned and strode purposefully out of the office.

Chapter 3

"You're a land speculator," Henry told him the next morning.

"I wanted to be a horse buyer," Longarm protested. "Worked all night on the stuff I oughta say."

"Never mind what you came up with, you're a speculator. See! I had business cards made up for you last night. The address is mine in case you have to mail something, and the telegraphic address doesn't look like it but it will reach us here at the office. Put a bunch of these in your bag and some in your pocket. They should pass for the real thing."

Henry opened a desk drawer and dragged out a canvas money belt. "Put this on under your clothes. You have twelve hundred dollars there in gold double eagles. That should suffice, but if you need more you can send a wire to your 'office' address and I can arrange a bank transfer. That would add to your bona fides if you have to use it, actually. But mind that you don't spend too much. You could get the boss in trouble with his boss, and neither one of us wants that."

"I'm with you so far," Longarm said around the stub of one of his wicked little cheroots.

"Here's your train ticket as far as Lamy. Get off the train there and take a stagecoach east and south, down to the east-west road. Change coaches there . . . you'll have to pay for your ticket with cash, not a voucher, remember . . . and go west to Sand Springs. I couldn't find out much about the town, but it seems to be a major stopping place for stage-coach traffic in both directions. Once you are there, you can poke around however your nose leads you."

Billy Vail emerged from his office, where he had apparently been eavesdropping, and said, "Just keep in mind, dammit, that you aren't traveling as a deputy marshal. You're just another private citizen, so keep your nose clean and stay out of trouble."

Longarm gave the man a positively angelic smile and said, "No trouble, Boss. You know me."

"And that is exactly what worries me," Billy retorted before stepping back inside his private office.

"That should be everything," Henry said. "Good luck."

"Luck?" Longarm said. "Henry, I'm only goin' down there to look around. How much trouble could I get into just doin' that?"

"You, Longarm? I shudder to think of the possibilities. Now, get out of here before you miss your train."

Chapter 4

"Santa Rosa, Fort Sumner, and points beyond," the jehu called from the driving box of his light coach.

"Here," Longarm responded. He was standing on the Atchison, Topeka and Santa Fe platform in Lamy, carpetbag in one hand and newly purchased stagecoach ticket in the other.

"And here," a rather pleasant-sounding woman's voice said behind him.

Longarm turned and saw with considerable pleasure that the lady who was on her way to Santa Rosa was the same young and very pretty thing he had been admiring all the way down from Pueblo up in Colorado. Now it seemed he would be trapped inside a very small coach with her for the next day or so.

He could think of worse things than having to look at this blond and stylish creature. And he could think of better things than having to merely *look* at her.

He wondered what she would look like without those clothes. She was slender, and her linen duster concealed the details of her figure, but he had the impression that she might have high-riding, perky tits beneath all those layers of cloth. Longarm liked perky tits. Liked certain other things too.

He felt the first stirrings of a hard-on and quickly looked away. He tried to concentrate on things other than the blond woman. Looked at the four-up that would be pulling the coach down to the next relay station. Looked at the clouds drifting overhead. Looked at a piñon jay fluttering down from somewhere to examine a bit of discarded sandwich and peck at the scrap.

When he felt sure that his dick had subsided, he walked over to the coach. The driver accepted his bag and stowed it on top of the vehicle. Longarm took the lady's bag and handed it up to the driver. Then he assisted the blonde into the coach and crawled in behind her.

"Are you going far?" the lady asked.

"On down to Alamogordo," Longarm told her. "You?"

She smiled. She had dimples when she smiled. And perfect, blindingly white teeth. "I'll be with you to Santa Rosa."

He nodded. And wondered if Billy would mind if he laid over in Santa Rosa for a day. Or two. With a girl as pretty as this one it would be worth making some explanations. Or excuses.

"If you need anything," he said, "I'll be honored to oblige you, ma'am."

"You are very kind, Mr. . . . ?"

"Long," he said automatically. Then quickly realizing his error, since he was supposed to be down here as a traveling land speculator and *not* as a certain deputy whose name might well be known, he coughed and said, "Excuse me. My name is Lon Hippenmeier."

"I can see you are a gentleman, Mr. Hippenmeier. It will be a pleasure traveling with you, I am sure. My name is Samantha Morris, but you can call me Sam." She laughed when she said that, and extended a gloved hand for him to shake.

Longarm touched Sam's fingers and smiled.

This promised to be a most enjoyable ride south. At least as far as Santa Rosa anyway.

"Are you folks settled in down there?" the driver called.

Longarm raised an eyebrow and got a nod from Sam Morris. Then he leaned out of the window and replied, "We're all set."

The jehu snapped his whip above the ears of his leaders, and the coach lurched forward, iron-shod wheels grinding into the red earth and leather springs creaking as the vehicle began to bounce and sway.

Yes, sir, Longarm thought, this trip was going to be a mighty enjoyable way to make a living.

Chapter 5

Sam chattered away, friendly as a new pup, for the first forty-five minutes or so. Then her conversation wound down. She yawned and said a polite "Excuse me, but I'm tired. Would you mind if I try to take a little nap now?"

Mind? He would be delighted. Conversation is fine but has its limits, and Longarm's brain was becoming as numb as his butt after all the mindless nonsense that Sam had been spewing. The girl was pretty, but he was beginning to suspect that she was shallow.

He could not help wondering, though, if she talked like this in bed. He quietly smiled to himself. It was a question he would not mind exploring should the occasion arise.

The girl closed her eyes and slumped down in the corner of her seat. Longarm tipped his hat over his eyes and more or less did the same.

The bumping and bouncing of the coach kept real sleep at bay, but he did manage to doze a few minutes here and there.

The road wound in and out, up and down, passing through miles of rock and caliche, piñon pine, and scrub oak.

"Turkey Trot station coming up, folks," the driver called to them after . . . after Longarm did not really know how long, as he was fairly sure he had been lightly dozing part of the time.

When he opened his eyes, Samantha Morris was wide-eyed and wide awake. She sat primly, hands clasped in her lap, while the coach tossed her from side to side.

"It will feel good to get down and walk on solid ground again," she observed.

"Have you traveled much in the west?" Longarm asked. She shook her head. "No, not really."

"There should be coffee and sandwiches available at the station," he said. "Are you hungry?"

"Famished."

"Mind now, you won't have time for a proper meal. The driver will want to roll on again as soon as he gets his team changed and fresh horses in harness."

Sam smiled. "Thank you for the warning, Mr. Hippenmeier."

Longarm was grateful for the reminder. He had quite forgotten the name he gave her earlier. When he got the chance, he thought, he really should look at the business cards Henry gave him. He had no idea what name Henry had put on them.

The driver whipped his team into a run for their entry into the Turkey Trot station. He pulled the outfit into the yard with a flourish and a loud call, setting his brake a moment early and sliding the coach in with its wheels locked and the horses blowing.

Longarm winked at Samantha and said, "Showin' off a little."

She laughed and gathered her skirts.

Longarm opened the door and leaped down at soon as the outfit came to a halt. He reached up and handed Sam down safely onto the ground.

"If you need the, um, the . . ." he began.

"No, thank you. I'm fine."

The girl must have a bladder like a horse, he thought, if

she did not need to go yet. He, on the other hand, needed the outhouse, and if she was not going to use it, he damn sure was.

He hurried around to the rear of the station building, found what he needed next to a barn out back, and drained what was left of the coffee he had consumed on the trains down from Denver. Then he slipped in the back door of the station building.

The scene he found there was not exactly what he had expected.

Samantha, an older woman, and a man he had never seen before were backed up against a side wall while two young men with shotguns in their hands and flour sack masks over their heads were in the process of robbing them.

Sam's purse lay on the long table together with a man's wallet, a small pistol, two watches, a steaming jug of coffee, and a platter of sandwiches.

"Come join our party," one of the robbers invited. Longarm thought he sounded very young, although that could have been due to the flour sack slightly muffling his words. "Put your wallet on the table and get over there with the others."

Longarm's money, most of it anyway, was in the money belt under his clothes. But his badge and credentials were in that wallet, and he could just imagine the rampage these boys could go on if they were able to pass themselves off as deputy United States marshals.

"Go on now," one of them urged. "Hurry."

"No," Longarm said.

"What?"

"You heard me. No. I ain't gonna let you rob the young lady. Nor me neither for that matter. Now, put those guns down an' get the hell outa here."

"We're not fooling, mister. Now, give it up before somebody gets hurt."

"If anybody is gonna get hurt," Longarm said, "'it'll be

you, so give up and go away." His voice hardened. "And do it *now*!"

Longarm could not see the robber's expression, but he could clearly hear a gasp from inside the nearer one's mask.

The robber began to swing his scattergun to bear on Longarm's belly.

Chapter 6

Longarm's .45 was quicker than the young robber's twelve-gauge. Longarm ripped off two quick shots. The first hit roughly in the middle of the flour sack and snapped the fellow's head back. The second took him low in the side and spun him around before he collapsed like a marionette with its strings cut.

The robber hit the floor hard and did not even bounce. His shotgun, fortunately, clattered down without discharging.

The second fellow, possibly smarter than the first, did not waste time attempting to shoot Longarm. Instead, he jumped forward toward the people he had come there to rob.

He jammed the muzzle of his shotgun against Samantha Morris's back and shoved her out into the room without so much as glancing down at his dying partner.

But then perhaps he had seen enough of that already.

"Nobody move. Nobody. That means you, cowboy. I'll blow this little lady in two if you try anything. Believe it."

"Oh, I believe you," Longarm said. He smiled. Took out a cheroot and nipped the twist off with his teeth. He spat the twist onto the relay station floor and with his left hand found a match in his coat pocket and flicked it aflame with his thumbnail.

He drew smoke into his lungs and slowly let it out. Then, still smiling, he said, "Then what?"

"Huh?"

The other woman, presumably the station keeper's wife, rolled her eyes up and slumped to the floor. The man beside her knelt but made no attempt to revive the lady. Longarm suspected the fellow was just trying to get out of the way.

The robber, in the meantime, still had hold of Samantha, his shotgun jabbing hard into her back.

"I asked you, mister, what you figure to do after you murder Miss Morris. In cold blood, I might mention, and right before more witnesses than you got shells in that scattergun."

"I . . . I . . ."

"If you got any sense, sonny, you'll lower the hammers on that smokepole, lower 'em nice and easy, an' set the gun down on the table whilst everybody collects his or her things back where they belong. Then we all can sort out who you are and who your dead friend is so we can tell the local sheriff all about everything."

Longarm drew more smoke in and released it in a series of small, nicely formed smoke rings.

"Look . . . mister," the robber said, "all I want now is to get out of here. I'm going to . . . I'm going to take the little lady with me. She can get on Kenny's horse. I'll leave her . . . I don't know. Someplace. Not too awful far. I won't hurt her. But you got to put that gun down and let me walk away. Now that's the deal. Take it or I'll . . ."

"Or you'll what?" Longarm asked, his voice cold and his eyes hard. "Or you'll kill her? Fat lot o' good that would do you. She'll fall to the floor and I'll have an easy shot. You kill her and I kill you. Is that the way you figure it? Because that's for damn sure the way it would work out, kid. So just put the gun down, then we can all sit around and wait while somebody goes for the sheriff."

"I swear . . . I swear . . ."

"Give it up, sonny. You made a bad bet, but it's better to be in jail than in a coffin." Longarm cocked his Colt to have the easier and more crisp trigger pull than double-action firing allowed.

"No. I can't. Really." The would-be robber shook his head inside the flour sack mask, the movement shifting the crudely cut eye holes so he likely could not see much, if anything, in front of him, and he did not have a hand free to adjust the mask. One hand was busy with Samantha and the other held the shotgun.

Longarm could hear the growing desperation in the young fellow's voice.

And he did not need to see in order to pull a trigger and blow Samantha in two.

Sighing, almost reluctant, knowing it was anything but a fair fight, Longarm took careful aim.

And put a bullet roughly where he assumed the lad's ear would be.

Robber and shotgun both fell to the floor. The shotgun hit hard, the impact jarring one of the hammers. The gun fired, and Samantha collapsed, the robber's body softening her fall somewhat.

Chapter 7

"Christ!" the bystander muttered. Then he turned away and puked his guts out on the relay station floor.

Samantha Morris lay lifeless, the back of her head blown off by the accidental discharge of the robber's shotgun. A sticky, gray mass of brain matter spilled out of her shattered skull. Longarm guessed that was what had upset the gentleman traveler so. Hell, he himself was upset, and knew he was going to be a mite queasy for quite a while. Just moments before, Samantha had been a lovely young woman. Now . . .

From the direction of the barn they heard three gunshots, the dull booming slightly muffled.

"What's that?" the traveler asked, rising to his feet and wiping his mouth with the back of his hand.

"That would be the station keeper murdering our driver," Longarm said.

"But . . . why?" the man asked, obviously confused.

"They're all in on the deal together. I wouldn't be surprised if those two dead ones there are the sons o' the station keeper and his wife."

"How can you know a thing like that?"

Longarm snapped open the loading gate of his Colt and punched out his empties, then reloaded with fresh cartridges from his pocket. "You might've noticed that there's been a heap o' gunfire in here, but nobody's come running to see why. Stands to reason one o' them out there had a gun on the other. We know it ain't our driver, so that leaves the station keeper." He smiled. "See?"

"What are we going to do?" the gentleman asked.

"I'd say that you are gonna pick up one o' the guns that's laying around and keep an eye on the missus here while I go out and see what we can do about the station keeper."

The gentleman swallowed hard. But he nodded, then picked up one of the shotguns—not the one that had blown Samantha's head apart—and checked the loads before snapping the action closed again.

Good, Longarm thought. At least the man knows how to handle a gun, if only because he had hunted game with one in the past.

"Stay here," Longarm said.

Idly, almost in passing, he stooped down and pulled the flour sack mask off the first robber he had killed.

"Aw . . . shit," he mumbled. The dead kid was a girl, her long hair matted with drying blood now. She could not have been out of her teens. She still had freckles.

Longarm gave the station keeper's wife a hard look. "No wonder you fainted. She was your own kid, wasn't she? You and your man put her up to this, and she died because of your greed. You are an evil woman, and I hope there is a special spot in hell reserved for you. Is that one a girl too?" He motioned toward the dead robber lying underneath Samantha Morris's body.

The station keeper's wife did not answer. She turned her face away.

Longarm turned to go outside. The station keeper could not be far away.

Chapter 8

"So what's the take, Maudie? Were they rich?"

The man's voice came from just outside. Longarm stepped to the side, his Colt held ready.

"Don't come in, Anse," the wife shouted, suddenly rising from the floor and scuttling over to her dead daughter. "One of these sons of bitches has killed our babies. Now he's got a gun. He's waiting for you, Anse. He's right by the stove. Now he's moving toward the door, Anse. Be careful, honey."

Longarm moved to the other side of the room. The woman called out to her man every time Longarm changed position. It was obvious she intended to continue doing so until Longarm and the other traveler were dead.

With a shrug but no regret for this killer, Longarm walked over to the woman. "You gonna shut up now?"

She looked up at him with pure, hate-driven venom in her eyes. "Fuck you," she hissed.

Without warning he smacked the barrel of his Colt just above the woman's ear. The woman was flung to the side, knocked out cold.

"Keep an eye on her anyhow," Longarm told the gent who was supposed to be guarding her.

Out of curiosity, since he happened to be standing beside

the body now, he reached down and pulled the mask off the other robber. That one was a boy, perhaps twenty or so. One thing for certain was that the kid would not be getting any older.

With another shrug he went in search of the station keeper Anse.

He tried to recall the exact sounds he had heard coming from the barn. There is a distinct difference between the sound of a shotgun and that of a revolver. Longarm was pretty sure the man called Anse was armed with a pistol. And that was definitely to the good. There is something about facing a shotgun that even Longarm shied away from, but he would stand face-to-face with anyone armed with a revolver. He had confidence in his own ability in a shootout, but still, shotguns made him nervous. Anse, he thought, had a pistol.

Rather than try to sneak around, Longarm charged straight ahead, bursting through the door and dropping in a flying roll to end up lying sprawled on his belly with his .45 extended.

Anse, pistol in hand, was standing with his back to the wall, waiting for Longarm to come out.

As soon as Longarm appeared in the doorway, Anse fired. But he was expecting a man standing upright, not one down at boot level. Anse's bullets flew a good three feet above Longarm.

Longarm's answering shots had no such problem. His .45 barked three times, flame and white smoke pouring out of the barrel, heavy slugs battering Anse's chest and belly.

The station keeper dropped his gun, tottered forward four short steps, and collapsed.

Longarm came to his feet and reached down to dust himself off before he once again shucked the empty cartridge casings out of his Colt and reloaded.

Chapter 9

Longarm was restless. It had been a day and a half since George Fallon, the other traveler at the relay station, rode away to bring the law, and the bodies left lying in the building were getting ripe. And Longarm was long since tired of Maud Batterslea's lip. The woman lay trussed up like a Christmas goose but that did not stop her from cussing and complaining.

Early in the wait for Fallon to return she had satisfied Longarm's curiosity about something though.

"Your son," he said. "When he was holding Miss Morris hostage, he said something about 'Kenny' being dead. But the dead one at the time was a girl. She was named Kenny? Unusual for a girl."

"Her name was Kendra. Kendra Louise Batterslea, and she is dead thanks to you, you black-hearted son of a bitch."

That only set Maud off on another rant, so Longarm quit paying attention and went back to waiting for Fallon to return.

Two stagecoaches did come through, but he would not allow the drivers or the passengers to enter the station building. It was best to leave everything as it was, he felt, so the local law, whoever they sent, could work out exactly what had happened.

The drivers had to change the teams without assistance. The only times Longarm left the building were to use the outhouse and to make sure all of the horses had feed and water. Apart from those very welcome occasions, he sat in the station building drinking coffee and keeping a wary eye on Maud.

By the time Deputy Sheriff Jim Benedict showed up, Longarm was heartily sick of her. And of the flies that were feasting on the decomposing corpses.

When Benedict introduced himself, Longarm extended a hand to shake and said, "I'm Henry Ankrum," the name Billy Vail's clerk had given him. Longarm had had plenty of time while he was waiting to look at the business cards Henry had made up for him and to memorize his temporary name.

"Pleased to meet you, Mr. Ankrum," Benedict said.

"Where is Fallon?" Longarm asked.

"Who?"

"The fella that went to tell you about the dustup here."

"Oh, him. He had business someplace. Delivered the message and rode on. He asked if it was all right. I told him there shouldn't be a problem if he just made out a statement and left it. Which he was doing when I left the office."

Longarm nodded. He did not blame Fallon for not wanting to backtrack to the mess here.

"While I was waitin' for you, Deputy, I found some stage line forms and wrote out my statement on the backs of 'em. You can act as witness when I sign them." He grinned. "I don't think Maudie there would be much interested in helping," he said, hooking a thumb toward the woman. She was tied tight in a straight-backed chair and was not particularly happy about it.

"You son of a bitch," she snarled. "Jim, who are you going to believe, me or this lying cocksucker?"

"Why, I think I'll believe what I see on the ground here,

Maudie, and the statements of two witnesses, and those things tell me that you will be going behind bars for a very long time."

Benedict turned to Longarm and said, "There have been two other coaches that disappeared from this run over the past couple years. Maud and Anse said they never showed up here, so we looked for them elsewhere. Never did find hide nor hair of them though."

"What would you bet you can find the burnt-out frames of the coaches in an arroyo someplace within ten miles or so from this place. And I'd bet you never will find the bodies. They likely burnt up along with the stagecoaches," Longarm guessed.

"You know, mister, you could be right about that. I'll tell the sheriff what you said. Maybe he can authorize a search party or post a reward or something."

Longarm nodded. Those would not be his cases, but it bothered him when loose threads were left hanging. He hoped these locals would be able to work things out.

Surely, though, Anse and Maud and their murderous brood had been behind those disappearances just as they'd intended to be behind one this time.

"If you don't need me anymore, Deputy, you can witness my signature, then I'd like to crawl off somewheres and get some sleep. I been away watching over the bitch there much too long. Then I reckon I'll take the next southbound coach as comes through."

"That's fine, Mr. Ankrum, and I want you to know how much we appreciate your help. We never would have known about this gang if it hadn't been for you," Deputy Benedict said.

It took Longarm a moment to remember who the hell Benedict meant when he mentioned a Mr. Ankrum. He really did need to catch up on his sleep, dammit.

"Good night, Maudie," he said in as pleasant a voice as he could muster.

"Go fuck yourself, you bastard," Maud shouted back at him.

Longarm was laughing when he headed out to the barn to crawl into the loft and get some sleep. Hopefully without the flies that were crawling over everything in the station building.

Chapter 10

He was hot, tired, and grumpy when he finally reached Salt Springs, New Mexico Territory.

Not that there was very much of Salt Springs to reach. The town consisted of a half dozen shops, several dozen adobe houses, and one lone structure of any substance.

And that was a whorehouse.

"If you intend to stay anywhere around here, mister, the KW is the only place where you can get a room," the friendly stagecoach driver, Eli Jenks, told him when Longarm climbed onto the coach roof to collect his bag and leave the stagecoach. "KW stands for K. Wallace, though I don't know if the K is an initial for something else or the name Kay. Whatever he name is, K is . . . well, she's something special." The man laughed. "You'll see that for yourself."

"She lets rooms, does she?" Longarm asked.

The jehu chuckled. "Rooms and more. I think you'll find that almost everybody passing through here wants to stay at least one night at the KW." The chuckle turned into a laugh. "Except for the ladies. They tend to get back aboard the coach and roll on to some place else."

"Then this would be the right place to stay, all right." He winked. "This bein' the only place." He grabbed his carpetbag and climbed back down to the ground, then looked around again.

His first impressions from inside the coach had been correct. There just was not much to see or do in Salt Springs.

Except for the KW, that is.

Longarm reminded himself that he was here as a civilian, not a lawman. He was here just to watch and to learn, and he had to act like an ordinary gent with the possibility of doing . . . What was it Henry had put on those damn business cards? Oh, yes. He was here as a speculator in land and real properties, whatever the hell that meant. And he had to act like one.

He smiled to himself as he climbed the steps onto the front porch of the KW. It was just a damned good thing Henry had not made him out to be a traveling preacher or some such thing so he would have to act the part of a teetotaler. That would be a helluva thing, now wouldn't it?

Chapter 11

The KW from the outside was an ordinary, if rather large, three-story structure, sun-grayed and weather-beaten. It had the usual broad porch lined with rocking chairs and a wide entryway with double doors in which were set frosted glass panels.

Longarm tried the doorknob and found it interesting that the door opened to his touch, just the way a proper hotel entry should. Whorehouse doors were generally locked, to be opened only by the madam or her surrogate and only when the customer has passed an initial inspection. Entry to the KW was easy. And pleasant.

Immediately inside the front doors was a wide vestibule with benches on either side where a gentleman might remove overshoes or a coat. From there the visitor passed through swinging doors with frosted glass panels that matched the etched pattern on the front doors.

And inside that was pure opulence, halfway between the plush décor of a top-drawer whorehouse and the practicality of a hotel lobby. There was even a desk with a pigeonholed rack on the back wall for messages and a board with hanging room keys.

The difference was that the desk clerk was a woman. And quite the woman she was too.

Longarm was greeted by a busty redhead wearing a red silk kimono. When he got closer to the counter and could see behind it, it became apparent that the kimono was short, about the length of a man's shirt. It left the redhead's legs completely exposed. And he suspected that if the girl were to bend over, the garment would expose a hell of a lot more than just her legs.

He smiled to himself, wondering what he could do to make her bend over.

"Good afternoon, sir. Are you checking in?"

"Yes, I think so," he told the girl, dropping his bag and leaning on the counter.

"Would you please sign our guest register." She slid the heavy book over to him and brought out a pen and bottle of ink.

Longarm turned the book around so he could find the line to sign. He could not help laughing when he read some of the entries. Ulysses S. Grant. Saint Nicholas. Kit Carson. Daniel Boone. They all had stayed at the KW. Most of the guests simply signed with an X. A very few had written actual names that were probably their own. Longarm dipped the nib of the pen into the ink and carefully signed in as Henry Ankrum.

The redhead spun the book to face herself, glanced down, and smiled broadly. "Welcome, Mr. Ankrum. I hope you will enjoy your stay. You can find refreshments and . . . entertainment . . . through that door there."

She pointed and said, "I will have your bag taken up to room, um," she paused for a moment and looked down to something out of sight behind the counter, "to room number eleven."

The redhead tapped a bell on the counter and almost instantly another girl appeared from a back room. This one was young, skinny, and Mexican. The bellgirl came around to the front of the counter and picked up Longarm's bag.

She trotted across the wide lobby, up a curving flight of stairs, and out of sight.

"This way, Mr. Ankrum," the redhead said, holding out a hand for him to take.

Chapter 12

"Oh, my," Longarm exclaimed when he stepped into the KW's parlor/saloon/casino.

"Do you like it?" the redhead asked.

"How could I not like it," Longarm said with a smile. "It's just my kind of place." The smile turned into a laugh. "It's every boy's fantasy an' every man's dream, isn't it?"

"That is a very nice way to put it," the redhead said. "Now, if you will excuse me, Mr. Ankrum, I will leave you on your own." She bowed her pretty head, turned around, and went back to her duties at the front desk.

Longarm could not help but wonder if the redhead performed other duties at the KW as well.

In the meantime . . .

He stepped up to the long, highly polished bar and immediately liked what he saw. It seemed that the barman was no man at all, but a very attractive blond barmaid.

The girl was wearing a silk kimono just like the one the redhead wore, except the barmaid's was bright green. But just as short. The girl had legs that were long, slim, and shapely.

"I think I like this place," Longarm said when she stopped in front of him.

"Oh, we hope that you do. That is why we are here, after all."

"What's your name?" he asked.

"Sandra. What is yours?"

He told her. "And what's the redhead's name?"

"She is Janice. Are you interested in Janice?"

"Is she, um, available?" he asked.

"She will be after eight o'clock this evening. What is your room number, Mr. Ankrum?"

"Eleven," he said.

Sandra swiped at the bar with a towel, never mind that there was not the least trace of a blemish on it. "What would you like to drink, Mr. Ankrum?"

"D'you have one o' the better brands of Maryland distilled rye whiskey?" he asked.

"Oh, yes. We have two." She turned and picked up two bottles from the right end of a long array of whiskeys. "Would one of these do, sir?"

"I think I done died an' gone to heaven," Longarm said.

The girl laughed. "Which one then? Or would you like a shot of each so you can decide?"

He pointed. "That one will do nicely, I think."

Sandra uncorked the bottle and poured a generous measure into a glass. When Longarm tasted the whiskey, it went down as smoothly as if he was drinking warm air.

"Wonderful," he said.

Whiskey this good was too good to toss back. It deserved to be savored. "Thank you," he said, saluting the girl with his glass. Then he turned away and went to take a look at the gaming tables.

The KW offered nearly anything a man could want in the way of gambling. It also offered some absolutely stunning young women, in nearly every size and hue Longarm could think of. Tall and short. Busty and slender. White, black, yellow, and red. The KW had just about everything.

The girls were not pushy, he noticed. They wandered in

and out among the dozen or so guests, making themselves available but not being insistent about it.

All of this had to be expensive, Longarm thought. Including these girls. Yet no one had spoken a word to him about money. Perhaps he was supposed to already know what things cost here, but if that was the case, he was well behind the game.

Speaking of games . . .

He walked around for a few minutes, then settled on a poker table where they were dealing five-card stud for stakes that did not seem terribly high.

"Is there room for another?" he asked.

The dealer, a young woman with gleaming black hair and an olive complexion, smiled and said, "It would be our pleasure if you were to join us, sir."

Longarm set his glass down, pulled out a cheroot, and settled in for some of that pleasure.

Chapter 13

"Too much for me," Longarm said, turning his cards over and pushing them to the side. He scooped his money off the table and dropped the coins into a pocket without bothering to count it. He had been keeping a casual count during the play and thought he was down about twenty dollars. Not too bad, he thought, for a pleasant evening's entertainment.

Still no one had asked him for any payment, not for his room and not for his drinks. Perhaps the KW made its money from the gaming tables. Unlikely, he thought, but possible.

Not that it was something he needed to worry about, he thought with a shrug.

Longarm picked up his glass and tossed down the contents. Damn, but they served a nice rye here.

He headed up to room number eleven. Found it at the end of the hall and let himself in.

The room was pleasant. And then some. It was also occupied.

Longarm checked his room key to make sure he was in the right place. Then he walked over to the bed, where a fan of bright red hair spread over the pillow.

He paused to light a cheroot, then turned the lamp wick

higher. And smiled. He sat on the side of the bed and began kicking off his boots. "Good evening," he said around the cheroot that was locked between his teeth. "Janice, isn't it?"

The redhead laughed and pushed the sheet down to her waist, exposing creamy white mounds of tit, each topped with a large, pink nipple, each already erect.   .

Longarm could see a tracery of purple veins lying beneath the milk-white skin of Janice's tits.

The girl pressed a hand beneath each tit and lifted, as if offering them up to him.

"Pretty," he said with a smile, standing and beginning to strip off his clothing.

Janice pushed the sheet farther down to expose a nest of curly red hair and pale pink pussy lips. She was moist, dripping wet, so much so that Longarm suspected she had been pleasuring herself while she waited for him to arrive.

"Even prettier," Longarm said, dropping his balbriggans onto a chair.

"Oh, my," Janice exclaimed when she saw the size of his now erect cock. "Now *that* is pretty."

Longarm was smiling too when he climbed in under the sheets.

Chapter 14

Longarm knelt between Janice's legs. He lifted her butt and hooked her legs over his shoulders. With the girl's ass high off the bed, he plunged into her. Deeper than if he had been lying on top of her. Janice gasped as he filled her, the head of his cock bumping up against something deep inside her pussy.

"Did I hurt you?" he asked.

"Never mind. Just . . . fill me. Oh, God." She whimpered a little and rocked her hips, pivoting around his cock. "So good," she whispered. "So nice."

Longarm pulled back a little and began to stroke slowly in and out. He took one blue-veined tit in each hand and increased the rhythm of his strokes.

Janice closed her eyes and placed her hands over Longarm's on top of her tits. She squeezed. Hard. He responded by lengthening his strokes and making them faster until he was ramming hard against her, his balls swinging free and slapping against Janice's asshole.

She cried out and he could feel her pussy contracting tight around his cock.

Longarm let go then, allowing his cum to gather deep in his balls and come spewing out with a rush. He could feel the flow as it spat up through his cock and out, deep inside her body.

With a grunt of pleasure he lowered her legs off his shoulders and let her pretty ass down onto the bed.

Longarm followed, relaxing and lying on top of the girl. He buried his face in Janice's red hair. He could smell her perfume and the soap she had used to wash her hair.

"You, my dear," she said, "are very good. I don't usually come like that when I am, um, working. But with you . . ."

She played her tongue around his ear, and Longarm felt his cock stir and become hard again.

Janice chuckled. "What *do* we have here, sir?"

"Sir?" he asked.

"With you it is a term of endearment, not a formality. Do you mind?"

"Not if ya put it that way," he said.

"You are hard again," Janice said.

"Is that a question?" he asked.

She laughed and reached down between their bodies to take hold of him. "Not hardly," she answered.

After a moment she shoved his chest with her free hand. Longarm rolled off of her and stretched out on the bed beside her.

"Would you mind?" she asked.

"Mind doin' what?" he said.

"This." With an impish smile she wriggled down at his side, then propped herself up on one elbow.

She leaned over his body and took the head of his cock into the heat of her mouth. She sucked him for a moment, then released him. "Do you like that?" she asked.

"Doesn't every man like that?" he answered.

"You might be surprised," she said. "Some don't."

"Then they're idiots," Longarm said, laughing.

"That's all I need to know," she said, taking him back into her mouth and once again sucking him, rolling her tongue around the head while his cock remained in her mouth. Her free hand toyed with his balls while she sucked. The tip of one finger ran around and around the rim of his asshole while at the same time her tongue was running around the head of his cock.

The combined sensations had the intended effect, and within moments Longarm could once again feel the sweet gather and burst of hot cum spraying into Janice's willing mouth.

She stayed with him, sucking until he was depleted. And exhausted.

Longarm was smiling when he rolled onto his back and dropped into a deep and restful sleep.

Chapter 15

Janice left well before dawn. Longarm stayed in bed until he could hear the bustle and clang of activity in the kitchen below. Then he got up, washed, shaved, and dressed, taking his time about it.

He ambled downstairs about half past eight and had a leisurely breakfast. Afterward he went outside onto the front porch and sat in one of the rockers while he smoked a cheroot.

At least two stages came and went while he sat out there, and gentlemen left both coaches to come inside for the delights offered by the KW, while others who had stayed overnight checked out and climbed into the coaches.

It seemed the KW did one hell of a fine business from travelers passing through tiny Salt Springs.

And thinking of business, Longarm realized, it was about time he paid some attention to his.

He went inside and asked the young woman behind the hotel desk, "Where can I hire me a horse or a rig around here, miss? I need some local transportation."

"That request is not unusual," the strawberry blonde assured him. "I'll see what I can do for you right away. Would you prefer a buggy or a saddle horse, Mr. Ankrum?"

"A saddle horse would be better, I think, for I might be wantin' to go places where there ain't no roads."

The girl smiled and said, "Why don't you wait in the casino while I make the arrangements."

"Yes, ma'am," he said.

The casino was as busy at this morning hour as it had been last evening, he noticed. He recognized among the gents at the gaming tables the men who had arrived only that morning, along with others who had been there the night before. Several of those looked like they had not quite gotten around to going to bed yet.

Another thing he noticed was that there were no windows in the big casino room. If he had not known it was broad daylight outside, he could not have guessed it from in here.

Smart, he thought. Keep the play going around the clock.

He walked over to the bar and propped himself up there.

"What can I bring you, Mr. Ankrum?" the girl behind the bar asked, a blonde in a pink kimono but not the same blonde who had been on duty there the evening before.

Make it a point to know the customers by name, he noticed. Make everyone feel quite at home and comfortable. Taking that trouble would likely pay off in the end.

"Can I get a coffee here?" he asked.

The pretty girl smiled. "You can get almost anything here, Mr. Ankrum. Including coffee. Wait just a moment. I'll have some brought over from the dining room."

He nodded and turned to watch the play on the casino floor. And the players.

His coffee was delivered in no more than two minutes, complete with cream, white sugar, and honey if he so desired.

And still not a word had been said about payment for any of it.

Longarm was on his third cup of coffee when a slender Mexican girl wearing a cotton dress and huaraches found him.

"Your horse is ready, Señor Ankrum. It is outside, sir. It is the dark gray with vaquero saddle." She smiled. "You will like this horse, I think. Very smart horse and steady."

"Thank you."

He started to tip the girl, but she waved his coin away. "That is not necessary, señor." She turned and moved lightly away before he could protest.

Chapter 16

The horse turned out to be a dappled mare, so dark a gray as to look almost purple. Her mane and tail were pale almost to the point of being white. The saddle that the girl had said was a vaquero saddle was a Mexican rimfire rig with a soup-bowl saddle horn. The important point from Longarm's view of things was that the suede seat was comfortable as an old shoe, and the mare proved to be comfortable as well.

He checked her mouth. The bit hanging there was a snaffle, suggesting she did not need a strong hand on the rein. Her age was perhaps twelve or fourteen. Certainly she was no youngster.

Her legs were sound, though, and her shoes almost new and well set.

He stepped into the saddle, prepared to ride out some shenanigans if the mare offered any, but she stood quiet and calm.

Longarm touched a spur to her flank, and the horse moved out into a swift and comfortable extended walk.

He had no idea where he was going, of course, but he wanted to convey the impression that as a land speculator—it was what his business cards claimed him to be anyway—he would be out there looking at land.

So he rode south out of Sand Springs and looked at land. Not that there was so much to see, mostly dry scrub and some rock formations. All in all there seemed to be little out there that would attract man or beast. The grazing would be poor and the mineral values nonexistent as far as he could tell. Not unless someone put a value on sand and caliche, cactus and rabbit brush.

Still he rode on for an hour or so, then found some shade under the cottonwoods beside a dry creek bed. He supposed the creek would host some flow in spring. Enough to feed the roots of the stand of cottonwoods, anyway.

Longarm reined the mare in among the trees and dismounted, wishing the girl back at the KW had thought to hang a canteen on the saddle. As it was, both man and horse would have to do without for the time being.

He knew better than to allow a strange horse to wander on its own. Longarm was capable of walking back if he had to, but he damn well did not want to, not in the desert heat, or under any other weather conditions either.

He settled for loosening the forward cinch so the mare could breathe easier, then he found a patch of soft sand at the base of a tree, the sand free of goatheads or other irritants. Longarm sat down, leaned back against the bole of the cottonwood, and tipped his hat forward over his eyes.

He was just out here for show anyway, and there was no one around to show off for, so he might as well rest both himself and the mare while he stayed away long enough to make his explorations plausible for anyone who might take notice.

After all, he would not actually be buying any of this arid and mostly useless land.

He closed his eyes and let his thoughts drift wherever they might choose to wander.

Chapter 17

"Hey, mister, whacha doing out here all by your lonesome?"

Longarm opened his eyes to see a kid standing over him. The human kind of kid, that is, not a young goat. This kid looked to be seven or eight years old and in need of both a bath and a new set of clothes, as his were past being ragged.

The boy was holding a small rifle, one of the falling-block single-shot models produced by Stevens and a few other companies. In contrast to the boy, the little rifle was scrupulously clean and oiled.

"Don't shoot," Longarm teased, throwing up his hands in surrender.

"Aw, I ain't gonna shoot you nor rob you nor anything. I was jus' curious whacher doin' out here by yourself."

"Well that's good to hear," Longarm said, feigning relief. "Can I put my hands down now?"

"Sure, mister. Say, you still ain't tol' me why you're here."

Longarm dropped his hands to his lap. "Just passing time," he said. He smiled. "Listening to my belly rumble."

"You hungry, mister?"

"I sure am," Longarm said. "I came away this morning

without giving thought to dinner. Now I'm out here without any."

"My ma is an awful good cook," the boy said. "You could come have dinner with us."

"Say, now, that sounds fine," Longarm said. "You don't think she would mind you dragging home a hungry stranger?"

"Mister, I've drug home all kindsa stuff." The kid grinned. "She might think a grown-up stranger is a improvement for a change."

Longarm laughed. He stood up and brushed off the seat of his britches, then untied the mare and stepped into the saddle. He held a hand down to the boy and said, "Ride up here with me so you can show me the way, son."

The boy's eyes went wide with excitement. "You mean that? I can ride your pretty horse with you?"

"You can if you take hold o' my hand," Longarm said.

The boy handed his rifle up to Longarm, grabbed on to Longarm's hand and Longarm lifted him into the saddle. Longarm shifted back on the broad seat and put the boy in front.

"D'you know how to ride, boy?" he asked.

"Yes, sir. Well, sort of. I've rode sheep and calves in our pen, an' we have an old mule that I get up on when Ma isn't looking. But I've never . . . not on any horse as pretty as this'un."

"D'you think you can handle a set o' reins?"

"Oh, sure. I haf t'do that when I plow."

"A horse like this you neck rein, you don't plow rein. D'you know the difference?"

"Yes, sir, I do."

"Then here. Take us to your home." Longarm handed the gray's reins to the boy. He could only see the back of the boy's head, but he was willing to bet there was a mile-wide grin on the little guy's face as he took charge of the handsome mare.

The kid thumped with his heels so hard he was bouncing up and down in the saddle, but all his heels were hitting was the wide leather stirrup straps on the Mexican saddle, so without saying anything to the boy, Longarm touched his spurs lightly to the mare's flanks and the horse moved out.

Chapter 18

"Ma! Ma. Come out an' see," the kid called after reining to a stop in front of the tar-paper shack that was his home.

A painfully thin woman wearing a much washed house-dress stepped outside.

"Calvin. What are you doing on that horse?"

"Mister man here asked me to ride him, Mama. He said I could."

"Well get down from there right now before you fall off and hurt yourself," the woman demanded.

"I won't fall off, Ma. I rode this ol' horse all the way from the grove."

"Did you shoot anything with that rifle gun, Calvin? Did you make any meat today?"

"No, Mama. I'm sorry."

The woman looked up at Longarm for the first time and said, "I hope he hasn't been a bother to you."

"No trouble at all, ma'am. I've enjoyed getting t'know him," Longarm said.

"I told this mister that he could get a lunch here, ma, 'cause he didn't bring none of his own." The kid's tone of voice suggested he was not entirely sure the invitation would be honored.

"Calvin! You did *what*?"

"I tol' the mister—"

"I heard you the first time, Calvin," the woman snapped.

Longarm could hear a baby begin to cry inside the shack. "Ma'am, I don't mean t'put you out. I'd thank you for a drink o' water for me an' for the horse, then I'll be on my way."

"Lawsy, I've complete forgot my manners, mister. Of course I can feed you. We haven't much, but you are welcome to share what there is," the woman said. "Now, Calvin, get down from that animal and go see to your brother."

"Yes, ma'am." The boy slid down off the mare and reached back up for his rifle—it was a .32-20, Longarm had noticed on the way from the grove—and dashed inside.

"The well is over there," the woman said. "Help yourself."

"Thank you, ma'am." Longarm tipped his hat to the woman, then stepped down.

He led the mare into a pen that was shared by half a dozen lop-eared goats and stripped the saddle and bridle off the horse. He spent several minutes filling a water trough that the family had allowed to go empty—the goats rushed in so quickly and drank so much he had to fill it twice—then quickly washed his face and hands before presenting himself at the house.

"Our name is Thomas, mister. I am Mae Thomas. You already know my firstborn. The next oldest is Timothy. The baby in the basket is Elizabeth," she said as she led Longarm inside.

"An' I'm, uh . . . my name is Ankrum, Mrs. Thomas. Henry Ankrum." He remembered the lie barely in time to avoid blurting out his true name.

"I suppose you're staying at that den of sin up in the city," she said with a sniff.

Longarm almost laughed out loud at the notion that tiny Salt Springs would be called a city. "Yes, ma'am, I am, it bein' the only hotel hereabouts."

"Sodom and Gomorrah, Mr. Ankrum. That is what that city is, Sodom and Gomorrah, both rolled into one. Sit down, Mr. Ankrum. At the table there. I'll have some food on the table in short order."

"Yes, ma'am. Thank you." He removed his hat and saw an empty peg on the wall where he could hang it. A peg where a Mr. Thomas should hang his hat if there was a mister in this house.

Longarm put his Stetson there, then took the offered seat. He did not want to be obvious about it, but he looked around a bit.

Calvin was behind a blanket that had been hung like a curtain. The little brother—Longarm could not remember the kid's name although Mae Thomas had mentioned it—seemed to be in there with his older brother.

The baby was lying in a basket close by the stove, waving her arms and kicking skinny legs and crying. Mae Thomas picked her up, slipped one tit out, and put the little one there to suckle while Mae ladled a mess of speckled beans into a bowl. She brought the wooden bowl and a horn spoon to the table and set them before Longarm.

"There you go, Mr. Ankrum."

"What about yourself and the boys?" he asked.

"We already et, thank you for asking."

Longarm doubted that. Doubted as well that there would be enough for them after he had eaten. Yet it would be poor manners to refuse the woman's food now.

He picked up the spoon and dug in. The beans were laced with diced chili peppers and tasted better than he'd expected.

"More?" Mae Thomas asked when he was finished. The tiny girl was still on her mother's breast, noisily sucking.

"Thank you, ma'am, but I'm full up." He smiled, softening the lie. He could have eaten three more bowls of the beans, but then the family would have gone hungry this evening, he was sure. "What can I pay you for my fine meal, ma'am?"

Mae looked startled. "Pay? You don't pay me anything, Mr. Ankrum, not for simply doing my Christian duty of feeding a stranger."

"Why, thank you, ma'am. You are a charitable lady, and I appreciate you. But I would like to pay you a little something."

"No, sir. Not a penny. That would not be right."

"As you wish, ma'am." Longarm slid his chair back and scratched his stomach. When he did that he surreptitiously extracted a twenty-dollar double eagle from his money belt and put it underneath the now empty bowl.

"If you would excuse me, ma'am, I'll be getting on my way now." He got the hell out of there quickly, before Mrs. Thomas might discover what he had done and make a fuss about trying to return it.

Chapter 19

Longarm saw a dozen or so longhorn beeves clustered near the grove where he had stopped earlier. Most of them scattered like quail when he rode near, but two of the creatures stayed to stare at him. Longarm drew his .45 and shot the fatter of the two squarely between the eyes.

The steer dropped instantly, the other wheeling about and racing off after the others.

Longarm shook out the reata that had come with the Mexican saddle and dropped a loop over the horns of the steer. It did not take much skill, seeing as how the horse was standing over the dead steer at the time. Still, what he was looking for was function not fancy form. It got the job done nicely.

He took a wrap around the broad saddle horn and dragged the dead steer back into the Thomas farmyard.

"I made a mistake out there," he lied when Mae Thomas came outside. "Thought this critter was a deer an' knocked it down. I don't want the meat t'go to waste so I brung it here. I hope you can get some use out of it."

He stepped down and first retrieved the reata, coiled it, and returned it to the saddle. Then he brought out his pocketknife. Leaning down over the dead steer, he carefully removed a piece of the hide where a brand had been burned.

"What are you doing?" Mae asked.

"Takin' this for evidence so's they can figure out whose animal this was."

The woman stared at him for a moment, arms crossed over her meager chest, then said, "You're an honest man, Mr. Ankrum."

"I try," he allowed. "Don't always succeed, but I do try."

"I shall pray that you have blessings, Mr. Ankrum."

He smiled. "When you come right down to it, I reckon I would have to say that I've been blessed far more'n I deserve, and I'll thank you for them prayers."

"And I thank you for what you left on the table earlier, Mr. Ankrum. It was kind of you."

Longarm did not know what to say to that, so he settled for tipping his hat to the lady and stepping back onto the horse.

It was not strictly kindness that had brought him here. He had a use in mind for that piece of cowhide with the brand on it.

"Good day, ma'am, Calvin." The boy was standing behind his mother, the somewhat battered little .32-20 in his hands.

Longarm turned the dappled mare and headed back north to Salt Springs.

Chapter 20

"Where can I find the town marshal?" Longarm asked of a fellow walking on the boardwalk in front of a general mercantile.

The gentleman stopped, turned to Longarm, and said, "We don't have a marshal of our own, but there's a county deputy that lives here. He generally handles any lawing that needs doin'."

"All right then, where can I find him?" Longarm asked.

"Down that way." The local man pointed. "Last house on your right. His name is Ricardo Gomez."

Longarm touched the brim of his Stetson and thanked the man, then gigged the mare into a walk in the direction the gent had indicated.

The house was a rambling adobe structure with a beehive oven in one side yard and a low adobe wall forming a corral on the other side.

Longarm stepped down from the saddle and stood for a moment, looking for a place to tie the mare since there was no hitch rail or hitching post in front of the house.

"I know that horse," a voice came from the shadows inside a front window. "She'll stand ground tied if you just drop the reins."

"All right, if you say so," Longarm called back to the man. He smiled and added, "But if she wanders off, you go find her."

"If she did wander," the voice said, "which she won't, but if she did, the worst she'd do would be to head back to the livery and that's not a hundred yards west of here."

Longarm fetched his rolled-up patch of fresh cowhide from behind the saddle before he let go of the reins. The mare stood ground tied as steady as if she was chained to a stout tree.

"I'm impressed," he said toward the window. He was, too. He took the hide, with the brand plainly visible, toward the house and said, "I'm looking for Deputy Gomez."

"That's me," Gomez said from his doorway. "Do you have business with the law?"

"I'm afraid that I do, Deputy." Longarm finally got a look at the deputy sheriff. The man turned out to be smaller than Longarm had expected, with steel-gray hair that suggested his age would be fifty or more. His face was heavily cratered with pockmarks. He stepped outside and offered his hand.

"I'm Henry Ankrum," Longarm said.

"What can I do for you, Mr. Ankrum?" Gomez hooked his thumbs behind his suspenders and leaned against the front wall of his home.

Longarm unrolled the piece of hide. "This morning I took a shot at what I thought was a deer skulking in some thick brush. My shot was true, but the damn critter turned out t'be a steer. I cut this brand off of it and brought it right away to you, hopin' you would know whose steer I killed. Naturally I'll pay for the man's loss. I didn't do it on purpose, but I did do it and I'll stand good for it."

Gomez grunted and said, "The steer belonged to John Ferris. His place is southeast from here. I'm familiar with John's stock. They're mostly longhorns, long-legged sons of bitches. That steer you killed would be worth fifteen, maybe eighteen dollars. Can you pay that?"

Longarm fished another double eagle out of his britches and handed it to the deputy. "D'you think this will cover the damages?"

"I'm sure John will be glad to take that for his steer. What did you do with the carcass?"

"I saw a house down there where I shot the steer," Longarm said, "so I dragged it over there, thinking they could use the meat. Looked like I was right about that."

"The Thomas place?" Gomez asked.

Longarm nodded. "I believe that's the name the lady gave."

Gomez grunted again. "Mae Thomas can sure use some meat. Her husband up and ran off a while back. Now she's out there by herself with those children to raise. Since you've paid for the steer, that meat was yours to do with whatever you liked. I'd say it has all worked out for the best, Mr. Ankrum."

Longarm thanked the man and gave both the gold coin and the piece of cowhide to the deputy.

Gomez seemed like an honest man. But in a few days, Longarm intended to look up this John Ferris and find out if the payment reached him or went into Ricardo Gomez's pocket instead.

Longarm touched the brim of his Stetson and walked back over to the mare, which was standing exactly where he had left her.

Chapter 21

"I'm sorry, Mr. Ankrum, but you can't have Janice tonight."

Longarm raised an eyebrow. "I know she's not entertaining some other gentleman. I just seen her walk through here two minutes ago."

The petite blonde behind the KW's counter smiled and said, "It's not a matter of availability, Mr. Ankrum, but of policy. In order to discourage, um, shall we say . . . *entanglements* . . . our gentlemen guests are asked to vary their selections." Her smile flickered again. "I'm sure you understand."

"All right," Longarm said. "I wouldn't want to run afoul of your policies around here. I like the place too much to do that. How about you then?"

The little blonde's smile became even wider, which he really had not thought possible. "I am off duty here at eight. It will be my pleasure to serve you then."

"An' what is your name, darlin'?" he asked.

"Letitia," she said, "but everyone calls me Tish."

"All right, Tish. I'll see you after eight. I'm lookin' forward to it."

Longarm turned and headed for the casino, thinking what a pleasant duty this was. He must have been living right to draw an assignment like this one. Of course, though, it would be another matter if he had to pay for anything and put such a charge on a government voucher destined for the eyes of Henry, Billy's stickler of a clerk.

Longarm was again amusing himself with thoughts of Henry's reaction when he came upstairs several hours later. Tish was waiting in his room. She was fully dressed, perched on the side of his bed. When he entered she came rushing to him, wrapped her arms around his neck and lifted herself high enough to kiss him on the side of his neck.

"It is so good to see you," she said with an enthusiastic squeal. "Janice told us that you are very good, and comments like that are very rare. Mostly the girls don't say anything about our gentlemen except a warning now and then. For one of the girls to compliment a man like that . . ." She rolled her eyes and laughed.

"Now that's mighty nice o' you, Tish. Thanks."

She dropped back down onto the floor and reached for his belt buckle. "Let me help you out of those clothes."

Tish undid the buttons of his fly, reached in, and pulled out his dick. Her eyes became wide when she saw the size of it. She immediately dropped to her knees and began sucking him, leaving his coat and shirt for him to manage.

"You're gonna have to let go so's I can get my boots an' britches off, honey," he said moments later.

"Do I have to?" she grumbled in response.

"Yes, you have to."

"Can't I just . . . you know . . . can't I just get a wee drink from it first?"

"All right. But then you have to let go so I can get the rest of my things off."

Longarm turned sideways and backed up until he encountered the side of the bed. Tish never let his cock leave her mouth while he was moving about.

He sat down and leaned back, thoroughly enjoying being serviced by the enthusiastic little blonde. Longarm closed his eyes and allowed the girl to please him.

Chapter 22

Longarm gave Tish her drink of hot cum, then when she finally let go of him, he laid his gunbelt aside, kicked off his boots, pulled off of his trousers, and was able finally to step out of his balbriggans and toss them aside.

Tish poured water from a jug on the floor into a basin and brought it, along with a dish of soft soap and a towel, to him.

"Can I wash you?" she asked.

"Sure, if you want to," he allowed.

"Oh, yes. Please."

He motioned for the girl to go ahead. The water was cold, but he was accustomed to that. Tish seemed to genuinely enjoy his body. He doubted that she missed any of it, front or back, high or low. She even peeled his foreskin back before she very gently washed him there, and she was careful to scrub his asshole too.

"I intend to have my tongue there later, so I want you to be clean all over," she explained.

Only when Longarm was thoroughly—and most pleasantly—washed did Tish step aside and remove her sky-blue silk kimono to reveal a body that was tiny but perky and perfect.

She had small, pale nipples, a flat belly, and a bush of curly blond hair.

"Anything more'n a mouthful is a waste, or so the sayin' goes," Longarm said as he took one of her tits between his lips. Her tits were barely the size of teacups, but they were pointy and firm and he liked them just fine.

She had rubbed her nipples with something he could not quite identify. But he liked it, whatever it was.

"Oh, that's nice," Tish cooed while he sucked on her tit.

He slid a hand between her legs, Tish obediently parting them to ease his entry. Longarm put a finger up her pussy, then two fingers while with his thumb he played with her asshole. Tish quivered, her flesh clenching tight around him as she came.

"So nice," she whispered. "Would you please fuck me now? I'm ready for it."

Longarm obliged, his cock filling her. In truth he was surprised that a girl as small as Tish could take his length, but she managed without a whimper and came twice more before his cum finally burst into her.

Tish laughed. "It's all right. You can give your weight to me. I know you've been trying not to, but go ahead. You can't hurt me by lying on top of me."

Very reluctantly, he let himself down onto her small body. Tish giggled and wrapped herself around him with her arms and with her legs. She buried her face against his chest and sighed happily.

"You seem to enjoy what you do," he ventured.

"Oh, I do. Especially when I can be with a fine gentleman such as yourself, Mr. Ankrum. Some of the girls are really here for the money. But I like what I do. I get to meet the most wonderful people here." She hugged him tight.

"You mentioned money. That's the first time anybody has breathed a word to me about it. How do you make your money here?"

"Us girls are on a salary, like. We get paid so much each

week. I put mine away. One of these days, when I have enough, I intend to go somewhere, maybe in the East, and open a ladies' wear shop."

"What about the gentlemen?" he asked.

"Oh, they will pay. And so will you, when you check out, I mean. The charge covers everything."

"Do you get tips?"

Tish shook her head. "That would be against the rules."

"What if a gentleman can't pay?" Longarm asked.

"Then Miss Wallace files criminal charges against him. She makes them stick too."

"By way of the deputy sheriff?" he guessed.

"Yes, and let me tell you, it makes Mr. Gomez . . . that's our deputy here . . . it makes Mr. Gomez furious that the law makes him put those gentlemen behind bars." She laughed. "It really is funny when you think about it because Mr. Gomez is a prig. He hates Miss Wallace and he hates this place and he hates something awful to have to take those men in, but it's the law and so he does it."

"Gomez doesn't come here?"

"Oh, no. He's straitlaced and fussy that way. He wouldn't step foot inside the place except in the way of duty. Which is his loss. I know Miss Wallace would let him have any one of us girls. Any two of us, for that matter. And she wouldn't charge him anything for it, but he's married and strict Catholic and wouldn't dream of it."

Longarm rolled off the girl and reached for a cheroot and a match. He got the slender cigar alight and lay next to the girl on the soft feather bed, enjoying both her company and his smoke.

For damn sure, he thought, this was an assignment to die for.

He did not know how close to the mark he'd come with that thought.

Chapter 23

Tish was still sleeping when Longarm slid out from under the sheet that covered them. Moving as silently as he could, he dressed, then paused to consider the razor that lay in the bottom of his carpetbag.

He felt of his cheeks and jaw. He definitely needed a shave, but if he hauled out his soap and mug and brush to whip up some lather, he was bound to wake the girl in his bed.

Longarm did not want to do that. She looked positively angelic as she lay there sleeping so peacefully. She had looked anything but angelic all through the night, when she'd practically turned herself inside out—and for that matter upside down too—the whole night long.

Besides, he told himself, if Salt Springs had a barber, the man would be a good source of local information, and he was certainly in need of some of that rather scarce commodity. If that was really an excuse to allow the girl to sleep on, undisturbed, well there was nothing wrong with that.

Fully dressed except for his boots, he picked those up and tiptoed out into the hallway. He stopped there to stamp his way into his boots, then went downstairs.

"Mornin'," he said to the stunningly beautiful young lady behind the counter.

"Good morning, Mr. Ankrum," she responded, her smile sunny and her teeth exceptionally white.

"I'm wondering, is there a barbershop in town here where I can get me a shave this mornin'?"

"Yes, sir." She gave directions to the local barber, at which point Longarm asked, "And what's your name?"

"My name is Iris, Mr. Ankrum."

"Are you already spoken for this evening, Iris?"

The girl grinned and said, "I think I am now. If that is all right with you, that is."

"'Tis plenty all right with me, Iris. Do you get off the desk at eight?"

"Yes, and I am looking forward to it all the more now," the dark-haired, blue-eyed beauty said.

Longarm tipped his hat to the girl, then wandered outside and set off in the direction of the barbershop, a cheroot between his teeth at a jaunty angle.

Yes sir, he was thinking, this was one hell of an assignment, all right.

Chapter 24

"Just a shave this mornin', please," Longarm said as he settled into the barber's chair.

"If you don't mind me mentioning it, you could use a trim too," the barber, a balding man of middle years, said.

"All right then. The shave and a trim."

The barber covered Longarm with a striped sheet, then tilted the chair back and stomped on the pedal to raise it pneumatically. Longarm closed his eyes and wriggled a little until he was comfortable.

"You're a stranger here," the barber noted.

"Aye, I am. I'm in land speculation, down here lookin' to see what's available, anything I might be able to turn a profit on," Longarm muttered. He could hear the barber whipping up some lather in a soap mug, then soon he could feel the light, cold touch of the brush on his face and neck.

While the lather soaked into his beard, the barber stropped his razor, the man's strokes rapid and sure. But then he likely had been performing that mundane task for many years.

With the razor sharp enough to satisfy, he stepped closer and used his thumb to stretch Longarm's skin. The barber

had a feather-light touch with the razor. Longarm could hear
its passage over his flesh more than he could feel it.

The barber stopped every so often to wipe the razor on
a towel before he returned to the shave. All in all it was a
pleasant experience, Longarm thought, one that if the truth
be told he rather enjoyed.

"Are you doing any good down here?" the barber asked.

"Doing . . ."

He heard a small laugh and the barber said, "With your
land inspections. Isn't that what you said you are doing
here?"

"Oh. Yeah, 'tis. Say, I had occasion the other day to talk
with your . . . deputy, someone said he is, not your
marshal."

"Gomez, you mean," the barber said. "You're right that
Rick is a deputy marshal. We don't have a town marshal, so
Rick takes care of what law we need."

"What do you think of the man?" Longarm asked.

"Salt of the earth," the barber said. "You won't find a
better man anywhere than our Rick."

"He's honest?" Longarm asked.

"Huh. As the day is long. He's a Christian gentleman,
strictly straight arrow. Anything Rick tells you, you can take
to the bank."

Longarm grunted. "That's good t' know. Thanks."

"Hold still now while I shave your throat," the barber
said while he wiped lather off his razor again. "Last week
a gentleman tried to talk while I was shaving his throat.
Took me half a day to get all the blood mopped up, and I
think I may have left some in the cracks."

Longarm laughed. And shut up.

The local man's opinion of Ricardo Gomez was interesting though. Straight arrow, the man had said.

There was one more test Longarm intended to apply,
however. Just to be sure before he reported back to Billy
Vail with his impressions of Gomez.

Chapter 25

Hair cut and clean-shaven, Longarm walked around behind the KW to the little barn where his rented dapple gray was confined. He tossed two forks of grass hay to the gray, then found the bin where a grain mix was stored. He poured a full scoop of mixed grain for the horse, and while it was occupied with its breakfast, he gave it a rubdown with first a currycomb then a dandy brush. The horse's coat practically gleamed when he was done with it.

His morning obligations out of the way, Longarm returned to the hotel for a delayed breakfast. Afterward, on his way out to the barn again, he was stopped at the desk.

"Yes, Iris? What can I do for you?"

"I'm sorry to have to bring this up, Mr. Ankrum, but would it be an inconvenience for you to pay your bill now? We don't like our guests to owe too much." She smiled sweetly. "It's just policy, you understand, nothing personal I assure you."

"Not a problem, Iris. I'll run up to my room and get some cash. How much will it be?"

"Seventy-five dollars, Mr. Ankrum."

"All right. I'll be right back."

He was wearing the money belt, heavy with gold coins,

but he did not think it a good idea to drop his trousers in the KW lobby. Better to have a little privacy.

Longarm took the stairs two at a time and walked down the hallway to his room.

The door was slightly ajar, not at all the way he had left it a couple hours earlier.

Longarm palmed his .45, eased up to the door, and stopped there for a moment to take a deep breath.

Then he burst through the doorway with his Colt extended and an unnerving growl on his lips.

The sound proved to be unnerving indeed. The young maid screamed and dropped to her knees, muttering something in Spanish and clasping her hands in supplication.

She had been in the process of making up his bed with fresh linens.

And a growing wet patch on the floor suggested the girl had pissed herself when Longarm came charging in.

There was no sign of Tish now. She must have awakened and left while he was out. He wished like hell that she was here now to act as intercessor with the cleaning girl.

"I'm sorry. Sorry. Uh . . . I don't know the word for it in Spanish, but I'm sorry as hell that I scared you," Longarm said, his words spilling out one on top of another. "Here." He returned the Colt to its leather, reached into his pocket, and found a coin. He did not even look to see how large a denomination it was but just handed it to the girl, pressing the coin into her palm and squeezing her hands together to make sure she had it.

"I really am sorry," he said several times more. "Finish what you're doing. I'll, uh, I'll go down the hall to the bathing room to take care of what brought me up here."

Chagrined, he turned tail and practically ran out of the room and down the hall so he could have the privacy he needed to get at the money belt.

Chapter 26

He paid his bill, then returned to the barn to saddle the dark gray mare. He pulled the front cinch snug but buckled the rear leather of the rimfire rig so there was a good inch of sag in it. It would act to keep the rear of the saddle down only if the horse got into a real storm. In the meantime, hanging loose like that, it would not irritate her.

He checked the feet to make sure the iron shoes were properly set, then dropped the stirrups off the saddle and stepped aboard. The mare swayed a little when his butt hit the saddle, but she made no offer to buck, and when he touched his spurs lightly to her flank she moved out to a smooth walk. He liked her. The horse was a damn sight better under saddle than the hard-mouthed Army Remount Service animals he usually drew.

Longarm had no particular destination in mind since he wanted mainly to give the impression that he was looking at land in the vicinity—that was what land speculators were supposed to do, wasn't it—so he stopped at the café to buy a pair of sandwiches and a canteen full of coffee, then resumed his journey to nowhere in particular.

He had been south already, so this time he took the road west out of town. If he cared to travel that far, the road would

eventually take him to Las Cruces. Or to El Paso. One of
those, he was not quite clear on which.

Not that it mattered. He only intended to ride five or ten
miles out of Salt Springs and then find a comfortable place
where he could hole up out of the sun for a few hours. Hopefully without puncturing his hide with too many cactus nee-
dles while he tried to rest up from last night's exertions. And
from the ones he thoroughly intended to expend upon Iris
that evening.

Longarm had come perhaps seven or eight miles and was
lost in thought about the dark-haired beauty, a hard-on rag-
ing inside his britches to the point that he seriously considered stopping along the side of the road to relieve himself
of that burden.

His reverie was interrupted by a shout of "stand and
deliver" from behind a clump of cholla.

Longarm came awake to find himself peering down the
twin barrels of a large-bore shotgun and a pair of Winchester
carbines.

The road agents wore linen dusters that covered them
from top to the ground. Each also wore a flour-sack mask
over his head. The only things about them that Longarm
could see were their weapons. And those were all cocked
and held ready.

Worse, the trio was well dispersed so two were on one
side of the road and the third man on the opposite side. There
was no way he could expect to fight back without getting
blown out of the saddle.

"Unbuckle your gunbelt and drop it on the right side of
the horse," one of them ordered.

Longarm complied—unhappy about it but having no
choice in the matter.

"Now the derringer," the same voice ordered. Longarm
was not sure he would recognize that voice if he heard it
again. But he was damn sure paying close attention to the
sound as well as the meaning of the man's words.

Son of a bitch! he thought as he fished the derringer out and dropped it into the loose sand of the public road.

"You can get down now," the voice said. "Just stay away from those guns. If we have to shoot while you're on the ground, we're apt to hit the horse too, and that would be a shame, fine-looking animal like that."

Longarm grunted. And carefully dismounted.

"Now loosen your trousers," the voice instructed.

"What?" Longarm blurted. "You want my britches too?"

"We don't want the trousers, mister, but we sure want the money belt you got inside them."

The bastards knew about the derringer and now they knew about his money belt too. Shit!

"You can take it off for us," the voice said, "or we can take it off your dead body, mister. Your choice."

Longarm loosened his belt and unbuttoned his trousers. He was beginning to be a little peeved by these sons of bitches. But he unfastened the money belt and pulled it out.

"Just toss it down," the voice said.

He did. He hated it. But he did it.

The one who had been doing the talking reached up to where the brim of a hat would be, assuming he was wearing one beneath that mask. He touched the hidden hat brim with a nod of his head and said, "Thank you, sir. You are free to leave in peace now. We won't bother you any further."

Longarm could not be entirely sure that these men would not gun him down as soon as he tried to ride away. Still, there would be no real reason for that. They had already pulled his fangs. And pretty much everything else he owned as well.

He swung up onto the mare, and the voice spoke one more time. "We'll leave the gunbelt and the derringer a half mile down the road. Don't try to follow us, though, or you might get shot. Or something. Ride back toward town a mile or so, then you can turn and head west again. But keep it to a walk, will you. I'd feel real bad if I had to shoot an unarmed man this morning." Longarm heard a chuckle. "Yeah. Real bad."

None of the others had uttered a word, but the one man was more than enough.

Longarm reined the mare back toward Salt Springs and put her into a slow walk away from the trio of highwaymen.

Chapter 27

He had had better days than this one.

On top of everything else, he pricked his thumb with a cactus spine while he was retrieving the derringer from where the robbers had tossed it.

He checked the loads in both guns, but those had not been disturbed. His Colt and the custom-made derringer were both exactly as they had been.

Longarm tried to spot the robbers, but the bastards were long gone. Along with the money belt containing roughly a thousand dollars of the government's money.

He could replace the cash. After all, it was only money. And Billy Vail had already provided for the possibility before Longarm ever left Denver. But, dammit, how was he supposed to explain this humiliation?

In his trousers pockets he still had—he checked—sixteen and a half dollars. That was far from being enough. After all, it cost twenty-five dollars per night at the KW. Pleasant nights, it was true, but not cheap.

With a sigh, Longarm put the dapple mare into a trot heading west. To El Paso or perhaps to Las Cruces, he did not know which. It did not really matter. What he needed was a town large enough to have both a telegraph office and a bank. Which Salt Springs was not. It was sure to have a telegraph station, although probably not an actual office. More like a desk and a telegraph key in the general store. But there was no bank, and Longarm needed a bank to cover the draft he would be able to receive via the telegraph wires.

He also needed another visit with those robbers, damn them.

He needed to find those sons of bitches and put them in irons, every one of them.

But especially the smart-ass cocksucker with the shotgun. He wanted to look into the man's eyes—without the flour-sack mask over his head—and personally put the steel around that one's wrists.

He wanted the bastard to know who was taking him in.

Longarm found himself hoping that Ricardo Gomez would not collar that one before he got back from . . . El Paso or Las Cruces or wherever; he wanted that man for himself.

Longarm gigged the mare into a lope down the west-leading road.

Chapter 28

Toward sundown Longarm found a ranch house and rode into the yard, scattering a flock of chickens and a half dozen ducks that were foraging for bugs.

"Hello the house," he called, remaining in the saddle while he did so.

A woman wearing an apron over a shapeless, much washed dress came to the door. She had flour up to her wrists, and her hair was coming loose from the bun she must have fashioned that morning.

"Yes?"

"I'm travelin', ma'am, an' I got caught out unprepared. I'd like to buy a meal off you an' a place to sleep tonight. Your barn yonder would be fine for me an' the horse too."

"You say you can pay?"

"Yes, ma'am."

"You can set out in the barn then, you and your animal. I'll bring you out something to eat when it's ready."

"Thank you, ma'am."

Longarm led the mare into the barn and settled her in a vacant stall along with a good bit of grass hay and a bucket of clean water. Half an hour later, just as dusk was turning to dark, the woman's man came home along with what was either a grown son or a hired hand.

The husband grunted a scant acknowledgment of Longarm's presence but made no offer for the traveler to come inside and join the family. The two men took care of their horses, then disappeared indoors.

Minutes later the woman came out carrying a tin pail. "I put your supper in here. Scrambled eggs and sweet potatoes. I'll bring you out some more eggs in the morning."

"That's good of you, ma'am," Longarm said, taking his hat off and accepting the pail from her. He dug into his pocket and came out with a silver peso the same size and value as a U.S. silver dollar. "Will this cover what I owe you?"

"Oh, it . . . it's only Christian charity to feed a stranger. You don't really owe me anything," she said.

"You're very kind, ma'am, but I'd feel better about taking your food if you'd let me pay."

"All right then. If you insist." She snatched the coin out of his hand as slick as one of those chickens out in the yard pouncing on a june bug.

Longarm had not brought any sort of bedroll along, but after he ate he made do well enough by climbing into the loft and burrowing into the hay.

He might have gotten a more comfortable sleep except for the torment that came from thinking about Iris waiting in his room back at the KW.

Chapter 29

The road went to El Paso, not that it really made any difference. Longarm could conduct his business in either city.

Once he reached the town, he went straight to the telegraph office and sent his message to Henry asking for more money.

"Check back with me this afternoon," the telegrapher told him. "I'll get the message off right away. It should be in Denver inside an hour, what with the relays that will be necessary for it to get there. Then they will send a boy to deliver the message to your party." He shrugged. "After that, who knows when . . . or if . . . they will answer. But check with me this afternoon. That would be the earliest you can expect any sort of reply."

"All right, thanks." Longarm grinned. "Any idea where a man can get a decent meal close by? And maybe a drink?"

"There's a Mex cantina just around the corner. Best enchiladas you ever put a tooth to, and they serve a decent cerveza too."

"Which corner?" Longarm asked, smiling.

The telegrapher pointed, and Longarm headed in that direction after thanking the helpful fellow.

The café was not one he would have entered if it had not been for the recommendation. The place looked old and rickety and on the verge of collapse.

Still, the local fellow had said the food was good, and Longarm was there to eat, not to admire. He went inside and helped himself to a seat, by habit choosing a table where he could sit with his back to the wall.

Even though it was not yet lunchtime, the place was at least half-full. Longarm took that as a good sign as to the quality of the food there.

The waiter was a fat man wearing black trousers, white shirt, and a red sash. If he spoke English, he was able to hide the fact.

"Enchiladas. *Tres*," Longarm said, holding up three fingers. "An' a cerveza."

"*Tres?*" the waiter asked.

"*Tres*," Longarm confirmed.

The waiter shrugged and left. Five minutes later the man returned carrying three platters, each loaded down with an enchilada the size of a bowling pin.

He set the platters down with a clearly amused expression, but he did not say a word. Nor did Longarm, who acted like this was exactly what he'd expected. One of the platters was enough for a full meal.

Trailing along behind was a boy carrying a tankard of beer that must surely have been at least a quart in size.

Longarm could only laugh.

And dig into his meal, which proved to be even better than the telegrapher had suggested. He managed to surround the first two enchiladas but admitted defeat when it came to a third.

He still had time to kill before he could expect a response to his request for more money, and he needed to walk off all that good enchilada anyway, so he set out to stroll the streets of El Paso while he waited for Henry to come up with his resupply . . . after first talking Billy into the necessity for it.

Longarm paid—damned little considering both the quality and the sheer quantity of his lunch—and began wandering aimlessly through the neighborhood around the decrepit little cantina.

Chapter 30

First Merchants' Bank of El Paso. It was only three blocks from the telegraph office and should be perfect for cashing a draft. Assuming Henry sent one. Which Longarm certainly hoped and expected he would do. It was either that or abandon the assignment down here and take the next available transportation north.

With time left to kill before he could reasonably expect an answer to his wire, Longarm wandered over to the bank and let himself in.

It was a small bank, paneled with dark wood and with a cozy, homey feel to it. The clerk there could never in his life have seen Longarm before that moment and certainly did not know him, and yet the man welcomed him with a smile.

There were two matronly ladies waiting to see the teller. Longarm fell in line behind them, thinking to ask the friendly man whether he would be able to cash the draft against the telegraph company's accounts.

Neither of the ladies was anything much to look at, but they smelled nice and reminded Longarm—he needed such reminders every now and then—that there really was a polite and pleasant society where guns and crime had no place and where the most drastic thing a woman had to do was to decide which hat would best go with her dress.

He yawned and smiled and patiently waited his turn.

The first lady completed her business, whatever it was, and stepped aside to wait for her friend. That one called the teller Earl. Their conversation suggested that the lady and her family attended the same church as Earl and his.

A little bell over the door tinkled merrily, and two men walked in wearing floor-length linen dusters.

There was nothing unusual about that.

But there was something decidedly unusual about the double-barrel shotguns they exposed once they were inside.

"Everybody freeze," the lead man ordered. "If you move, you die."

The lady at the counter fainted dead away. Longarm caught her under the arms and lowered her gently to the floor.

Her friend had somewhat more mettle. That one drew herself up to her full height of perhaps five feet and practically snarled at the robbers. She clutched her handbag to her chest and gave the men a defiant glare.

"You," the first robber ordered. "Hand it over."

The woman did not say anything. But she did not relinquish her bag either. Longarm had been close enough to hear that she just withdrew twenty dollars from her husband's accounts, and she was not going to give it up.

"Give them what they want, Rose," Earl advised from his window. "Just . . . give it to them."

"Look, bitch," the robber snarled, "you either hand it over or I'll shoot you down dead."

He aimed his shotgun at the lady's more than ample bosom and the purse she was clutching to it, but she still did not budge.

Judging from her expression and the way she held herself stiffly erect, Longarm suspected she was terrified but trying not to show it.

The robber, Longarm noticed, had not yet actually cocked his shotgun.

"Leave it be," Longarm said into the tension that was building between the robber and the lady. "She don't have much in there anyway."

"I'll leave it be," the robber snapped. "I'll cut the bitch clean in two. And you too, asshole. I got two barrels here." He half turned his head and to his partner said, "Either one of them moves, Bob, you blow the fuckers away."

"Don't," Earl yelped. "Don't hurt them."

"We'll blow your ass away too, little man. Now, shut up and start piling that money on the counter there."

The man looked away again to say something to his partner. That was a mistake.

A fatal mistake.

Longarm palmed his .45 and put a bullet an inch or so behind the man's ear.

Bob did not fare any better. As soon as he dropped the first robber, Longarm turned his attention on the partner, who was fumbling for the hammers on his scattergun.

"Drop it or die fighting," Longarm barked.

Bob looked up, a stricken look on his face. And dropped the shotgun clattering onto the floor.

The first man, incredibly, was still alive. Dying, but somehow clinging to life.

The stubbornly brave matron looked at the blood that was pouring out of the side of the robber's head, and she too fainted, slumping to the floor with a rustle of starched skirts.

Longarm was in no position to catch her the way he had her friend, so he had to let her drop. He kicked both shotguns aside, holding his Colt on Bob, and said, "Now the belly gun. Get rid of it, mister."

"Yes, sir. Yessir, don't shoot." The fellow very carefully opened his duster, unbuckled his gunbelt, and let it fall to the floor with a thump.

"You. Earl," Longarm said. "Go get the cops while I watch over these upstanding gentlemen."

Earl seemed plenty willing to get away from the blood and the lingering gunsmoke. He hurried out from his teller's cage and left at a dead run.

The ladies were beginning to stir again, but Longarm could do no more for them. He had to keep an eye—and a gun—on Bob.

"Don't fret y'self," he advised the robber. "The cops will be here in a minute, then you can settle down in a nice, comfortable cell an' contemplate what you done wrong with this job."

He grinned and with his free hand reached into his pocket for a cheroot.

Chapter 31

"It was just dumb luck," Longarm said, not for the first time. He was getting tired of this bullshit. He knew he could cut it all off short if he just pulled out his badge and announced himself as a deputy United States marshal.

But he was supposed to be down here undercover, and, however unlikely, it was not impossible that someone from Salt Springs might be keeping an eye on him.

"Are you willing to sign a statement as to what you've told us, Mr. Ankrum?" the officious desk sergeant asked.

"Of course I am," Longarm retorted. "After all, it's simple enough. I happened to be standing there. I seen a chance to cut the bastards off at the knees, so to speak, and I took it. Ask those ladies. They'll tell you the exact same thing."

"Watch yourself, Ankrum, or you'll find yourself in a cell along with that Bob whatshisname," the desk sergeant snapped.

"Watch myself how?" Longarm came back. "All I did was my civic duty as a free American citizen. Now you're giving me all this shit. What's the matter with you?"

"I warned you," the sergeant snapped, rising and starting around his desk.

Longarm's chin came up and his eyes burned fire. "Come

ahead if you think you're man enough, asshole," he snapped.
He had had just about all he intended to take from this prick
of a public servant.

"Hold up there. Both of you." A voice came from the
inner doorway. "Sergeant, back off. You! What is your
name?"

"Ankrum," Longarm said. "Henry Ankrum."

The man in the doorway grunted. "Come into my office,
please, Mr. Ankrum."

"Since you ask so nice, yes, I will," Longarm said. He
walked around the sergeant's desk and joined the tall, broad-
shouldered man who had interrupted what was turning into
a inquisition out there.

The tall police captain closed the door behind them . . .
then grinned and clasped Longarm by the arms. "Custis.
Damn, it's good to see you. I gather you're using some other
name, and I know you have a reason. No explanations
necessary."

"It's good to see you again too, Dennis." He looked at
the gentleman's uniform and smiled. "I see you've come up
in the world since I was down here."

Dennis Heathfield chuckled and brushed at the twin bars
on his epaulets. "Handsome, aren't they?" he laughed.

"More to the point, Dennis, they're damn well deserved.
Congratulations."

"Thank you, Custis. Coming from you, that means a lot
to me. Without asking what it is that brings you to our fair
city under an assumed name, is there anything I can do to
help you?"

"Yeah, you can come have a drink with me. Your company would be all I might ask," Longarm said.

"You can consider that done. Nothing else?"

Longarm thought for a moment, then shook his head.
"Can't think of a thing past that drink. We'll set us down
an' talk a spell, and I'll tell you all about the deal that's

brought me here. Part of it, anyhow. I guess there's parts I shouldn't be talkin' about."

He was thinking about Ricardo Gomez and U.S. Marshal Ben Phillips. At this point he very seriously doubted that either one of them—certainly not Gomez—was involved in this thing. But until he knew for certain sure that they were not, it was better that he keep his mouth shut and finish the job he had come down here to do.

"What I can't remember, Dennis, is whether you owe me a drink or I'm owing you one," Longarm said.

"I don't recall for sure myself," Heathfield said, "but I know how we can work it out." The big man grinned and clapped Longarm on the shoulder. "First I buy you one. Then you buy the next round."

"That sounds reasonable," Longarm said. "Lead the way, friend."

Chapter 32

Longarm spent the night at a little no-name crossroads where the proprietor sold him a box of crackers and a chunk of salami and for a quarter let him sleep on a cot in a shed behind the store. He had slept in worse places.

The next day he made it back to Salt Springs and once again stabled the gray mare in the barn behind the KW.

"Mr. Ankrum," the girl on the desk said when he walked in. "We were afraid you left us or . . . something. We packed your things for you and put them in storage. Would you like your same room back?"

"That'd be fine. What's your name, miss?"

"I'm Eloise." She was a looker too, but all damn day he had been thinking about that missed opportunity, so he asked, "Is Iris working today?"

Eloise tilted her head toward the casino. "Iris is tending bar today."

Until eight, Longarm thought, suddenly looking forward to the evening.

He said, "Yeah, have my things moved back to my room, please," then wheeled and headed for the casino. And Iris.

After all, she was one of the conveniences that came with the room.

Longarm was in the process of getting undressed. Iris lay naked and lovely in the double bed, waiting for him.

He removed his gunbelt and hung it on the bedpost, close to his pillow, then sat on the side of the bed and kicked off his boots. Standing, he unbuttoned his trousers and pulled them off along with his drawers.

He was just untying his money belt when it occurred to him—he felt foolish to realize he had not thought about it before—that these girls all knew about the money belt.

And so had the robbers who'd taken him down on the road several days earlier.

Those bastards had known exactly what they were demanding when they stopped him and asked not only for the few dollars in his pockets but for the gold-heavy money belt as well.

They knew. And they had targeted him in particular.

So it was likely, one way or another, that at least one of these lovely girls at the KW was involved with the robbery gang.

Whether Kay Wallace was also in on the deal remained to be seen.

Not that the boss herself was often seen. Longarm had not yet met the woman.

But someone at the hotel was involved.

Longarm wondered if Ricardo Gomez knew or suspected as much.

But then he also did not yet know if Gomez himself was an honest man.

That was something he expected to find out soon, though.

He would make a point of it.

He looked down at Iris, so lovely. So deadly? He wondered if she or one of the other girls was involved with this gang of robbers, or were all of them?

It was a question he would not be able to answer tonight.

Longarm slipped under the sheet and lay beside her. The

girl practically purred as she came to him, clean and pretty and eager to please.

Longarm smiled. His questions could be put aside until tomorrow. He reached down to the tangle of dark hair at her crotch.

Chapter 33

Longarm had breakfast at the café, then walked over to the barbershop for his morning shave.

He waited patiently while three locals received their shaves and one of them a haircut as well. When it was his turn in the chair, he asked the barber, "Would you happen to know a gent named John Ferris?"

"Of course." The barber—whose name was Ike or Isaac, something on that order of things; Longarm had not been sure, listening in on the barbershop conversations—chuckled and added, "John doesn't come in here any longer. The man is bald as a boiled egg now. Good fellow, though, if that's what you're asking."

"It was, and I thank you for the information. Any idea how I can get to his place?"

"Sure. There's a wagon road leads right past it. The sign on the gatepost says it's THE GROVE. That's John's ranch. The Grove." The barber finished stropping his razor and began to whip up some lather in his soap mug. He spread a thin film of lather onto Longarm's face and picked up his razor. "If you want to get there . . . hold still now . . . if you want to get there, take the wagon road that leads southeast from here. It's, oh, ten, twelve miles, I'd say. I know because

I've been there. John hosts a turkey hunt every fall, and I've gone on those a couple times." The gentleman smacked his lips. "There's nothing like a fat turkey for the Thanksgiving table, you know, and John has a good many of 'em down there. Wild turkeys, not the pen-raised kind. Yes, sir, mighty tasty."

The barber leaned close and squinted, then drew his razor down Longarm's cheek.

There was nothing like a barbershop shave, Longarm thought, to set a man up for the day.

When he left Ike—or Isaac or whatever the man's name was—Longarm walked around behind the KW to the barn. He fed and watered the gray and brushed her down before he put the saddle on her and went looking for a wagon road that led southeast from Salt Springs.

And where, he wondered, were these salty springs that prompted that name anyway? He had yet to see any such, but there surely must be some. At least one.

Chapter 34

The right road was not all that easy to find, but once Longarm was on it the ride down to the Grove was simply a matter of following the twin track until he came to the sign the barber had mentioned.

Once on the property he found it easy to understand where the name came from. In addition to running some scrub cattle, John Ferris owned a large grove of mature pecan trees. Longarm suspected the man made his living largely from those trees.

He rode into the yard and found a stoop-shouldered old man working on the running gear of a farm wagon. The gentleman had a snow-white full beard, but as far as Longarm could see around the edges of his hat, he did not have so much as a single hair on his head.

"Would you be Mr. Ferris?" Longarm asked from the back of the mare.

"I would," Ferris said, rising to his feet and wiping his hands with a piece of flannel rag. He was a tall old fellow and had only a few teeth remaining in his head, but he showed them with a welcoming smile.

"My name is Henry Ankrum, and . . ."

"Oh," Ferris said before Longarm could finish, "you're

the fellow that shot one of my cows. Thank you for owning up to the accident."

"How did you . . . ?"

"How did I know? Ricardo Gomez came down here yesterday to tell me about it. And to bring the money you gave him to pay for it. You overpaid, by the way. That steer couldn't have been worth more than twelve dollars. Maybe not that much."

"You did get your money then?" Longarm asked.

"Oh, yes. Ricky made a special trip down to deliver it. He said he didn't feel comfortable walking around with someone else's money in his pocket, and he didn't know when he might see me otherwise. So he rode down here yesterday and delivered that coin. Thank you. Ricky told me what you did with the carcass. That was a fine idea."

"I'm glad you approve, sir," Longarm said.

"I very much approve. And after all, you paid for the animal. It was yours to do with whatever you wished. Say, would you like some pecans to take home with you?"

"Oh, I like pecans well enough," Longarm said.

"Then let me give you some. I owe you change from that twenty anyway. Let me give you a peck of my nuts."

"There's no way I could use a whole peck. A quart or two would be plenty."

"Easily done. Do you have a sack to carry them in? No? Never mind. I'm sure I can find something to put them in."

"You are very kind, sir," Longarm said.

"Not at all. Now, let me see . . ."

Longarm was sure after speaking with Ferris that Ricardo Gomez was indeed an honest man. He munched on a handful of pecans on his way back to Salt Springs and thought about Gomez.

He was certain about the man's honesty at this point. In all likelihood the gang of highwaymen deliberately lured Gomez away from their crimes so the man would not interfere with their plans. That let Gomez off the hook.

It also meant that Longarm's job down here was done. He had been sent to find out about Gomez, and he had.

But, dammit, he had also been waylaid and robbed.

The idea of walking away and allowing those sons of bitches to get away with that was just too much to swallow.

They obviously knew Deputy Gomez and were able to keep him from destroying their little game.

And just as obviously they had something to do with the KW. That was a little detail that Longarm doubted Ricardo Gomez had figured out.

Longarm could tip Gomez off to that fact and return to Denver now. Hell, that was what he was expected to do now that his assignment had been completed.

But . . . no.

Even if he had to pay his own way from this point on—a drastic measure but one he would take if he had to—he wanted to stay. He wanted to take this gang down and see every last one of the bastards behind bars.

He also wanted to get something other than his sack of pecans for his dinner. He bumped the gray mare into a lope on the road back to Salt Springs.

Chapter 35

Longarm considered finding somewhere else to sleep. That would keep him away from whoever it was at the KW who was allied with the gang of highwaymen.

It would also, of course, take him out of position to observe the people who worked at the KW. At least one of the employees there was involved with the gang, and very likely that person—or persons—would be among the girls.

Who else would have been able to observe Henry Ankrum removing his heavily laden money belt when he undressed at night?

Longarm figured at least one of the girls was involved. It was quite possible that Kay Wallace was also in on the deal. After all, the boss was the one who hired the girls, the one who was in charge of them.

Longarm was still thinking about that when he reached Salt Springs. He rode around to the back of the KW.

A young couple—he had seen the girl working inside the hotel; he could not recall her name but she was one of the available girls in there—were on the back porch, locked in the middle of an embrace. The young man, a cowboy judging by his clothing, had his hand inside the girl's kimono.

His trousers stuck out in front of him by an impressive distance.

When Longarm rode into view, the two jumped apart, and the boy's face turned red.

The young cowboy whispered something to the girl, then backed away from her, eyeing Longarm all the way, and jumped onto his horse standing ground hitched nearby. He gave Longarm the evil eye one more time, then reined his pony away and threw the steel to it. The wiry little horse threw dirt as it scampered away.

Longarm turned his head to hide a smile, dismounted, and led the dapple gray mare inside the barn.

He tied the horse, unsaddled and went into the tack room to hang his saddle and fetch out a hoof pick and a currycomb.

When he stepped out into the alley between the barn stalls, the girl was there.

"Yes, miss?"

"I want . . . I need to talk with you, Mr. Ankrum."

"All right. Mind if I tend to the horse while you talk?"

"No, of course not, I . . . You saw Kenneth and me," she said.

"I did," Longarm agreed.

"Kenneth don't know what us girls do at the KW."

"I won't tell him."

"Promise?" She had gotten worked up with her Kenneth kissing her and feeling her, and now her breath was coming quick and ragged.

"Sure."

"And . . . and . . . Miss Wallace? Will you promise not to tell her neither, for us girls aren't allowed to have boyfriends."

Longarm shrugged. "All right."

"Say it," she insisted.

"All right. I promise not to tell Miss Wallace about you

and Kenneth." He stopped working on the mare and turned to face her. "What's your name, girl?"

"I'm Louise."

It occurred to him that he might be able to use Louise. "Are you spoken for tonight, Louise?"

She looked startled. "I . . . You seen me with Kenneth. You know I'm sweet on him. It's him that I'm working for, for him and me to have us a home of our own. You seen that but you want me to come fuck you tonight?"

Longarm gave the girl a twisted smile. He knew what she was up to, but he wouldn't let on. Not yet. "Yeah," he said. "That's right. Probably have you suck me too. You can think 'bout Kenneth while you got my cock in your mouth if you like. Just don't tell me about it after."

"I think . . . I think . . . oh, shit," Louise mumbled.

"Eight o'clock, right?"

The girl's head was hanging, but she managed to nod before she turned away and walked very slowly toward the looming bulk of the hotel.

Longarm grinned. He began to whistle a tune when he returned to grooming the mare prior to turning her into a stall and feeding her.

But then it was Henry Ankrum who was being a son of a bitch here, not Custis Long. But only Custis Long knew why.

Chapter 36

Longarm treated himself for dinner. He ordered a whole roasted duck along with red-jacket potatoes, sweet corn on the cob, and a truly exceptional peach compote. Afterward he headed into the casino for a glass of whiskey and a run at the cards. Two hours later he was ahead by almost fifty dollars. And it was after eight o'clock.

His room was empty when he reached it. The bed was freshly made up and there was water in the jug, but there was no sign of Louise. He sat on the side of the bed and smoked a cheroot while he considered going downstairs for another whiskey.

Then he heard a very light tapping on his door.

Longarm laid his hand on the butt of his .45 before he called, "Come in." He was not expecting any trouble. But then it was better to be prepared and have no trouble than to have trouble find you unaware.

The door opened a matter of inches . . . and Louise peeped in.

Longarm gave the girl a flinty stare. It was a look that had weakened the knees of a good many hard cases over the years. Little Louise was no match for it. She stepped inside and immediately started to bawl, snot running from her nose and her complexion turning red.

"Close the door."

Trembling, the girl did as she was told.

"Lock it."

She slid the bolt in place.

"Stand right here." He pointed to a spot by the foot of the bed.

"Take off your clothes."

She was wearing only her kimono and a pair of panties. Those quickly hit the floor.

The body that Kenneth was so fond of was nothing exceptional. Louise had high-riding, pear-shaped tits, a slightly too wide ass, and a little too much belly for Longarm's taste. Because the cowboy was so fond of them made it somehow harder for Longarm to do this.

"Are you fucking Kenneth?" Longarm asked. "Or just the customers here at the hotel?"

"J-just . . . the men here," Louise babbled. "Kenneth, he thinks I'm a virgin. He's felt of me, but that's all we ever done, him and me. Just . . . touching. You know?"

"But with the customers here you do whatever they want, is that it?" Longarm asked.

Louise nodded, her tears falling even faster now. They dripped off her chin and onto her chest.

"What do you tell Miss Wallace about the customers?" he asked.

Louise looked up, obviously puzzled by the question. "Miss Wallace? Why would I tell her anything about what the gentlemen ask me to do?"

"Not what they want, but what you see," Longarm said.

"I don't understand," the girl said, her lower lip trembling and her breathing ragged.

"Does Miss Wallace want to know anything about your customers? What they have in their pockets, for instance? Or their money belts? Pretty much every traveling man wears a money belt or some such thing, doesn't he? You would see that when the men get naked. You could tell Miss Wallace about it."

"I . . . I don't know about anything like that," Louise said.

"You're lying," Longarm snapped, his voice hard as steel and cold as ice.

"No, I . . . no. I'm not."

"Then who do you tell about what you see in a gentleman's room?"

"I can't tell you that," she wailed. "He would kill me if I said anything."

"And I might kill you if you don't," Longarm said. "At the very least I would make sure Kenneth knows what you and the other girls do here at the KW, and I would make sure that Kay Wallace knows about your sweetheart."

"Please," Louise pleaded. "Please don't do that. Kenneth . . . the home we want to build . . . he would leave me. I know he would if he ever found out about . . . what I do. I told him I'm a housemaid. Please, Mr. Ankrum, don't tell him no different."

"You have to tell me who you report to about your customers," Longarm insisted.

"I can't. I mustn't. Please."

Longarm already felt like the sorriest son of a bitch who ever walked the surface of the earth, but he knew he had to make it even harder on the girl.

"Hit your knees, bitch."

Chapter 37

When he went down to breakfast, Longarm was still feeling like he was the one who put a turd in the punch bowl. He might just as well have put a gun to the girl's head. Worse, he might have to pull the trigger.

He had given Louise three days to think it over before he would ruin her life. Or so she believed, anyway. Three days to cry and to worry.

The thing was, what the hell was he supposed to do if Louise was so fearful that she did *not* tell him everything she knew about the gang of robbers?

It was bad enough *acting* like a bastard. He could not actually do it. He knew that. Whatever Louise did—or did not do—he did not intend to tell her Kenneth that his intended was a whore, nor would he say anything to Kay Wallace about Louise having a boyfriend.

But there was no way he was going to let Louise know. He still wanted to squeeze that information out of her.

Now she had three days of fear and trembling to deal with, the poor kid.

Longarm's appetite was not good after a night of being such a son of a bitch, but he forced down a bowl of oat porridge and half a dozen cups of strong coffee before he ventured beyond the walls of the KW.

He walked over to Salt Springs' only general mercantile and bought a handful of cheroots. They were a little dry and brittle and not as good a taste as his own favorite brand that he could find back home in Denver, but they were a passable smoke.

With a sigh, Longarm remembered that he was supposed to be a land speculator out looking for land, while this morning all he had done was to mope around town. That would not do.

He added a box of .45s to his purchases and returned to the KW and around back to the stable where he was keeping the mare. Within a few minutes she was saddled and they were on the road, heading nowhere in particular.

Chapter 38

Without particularly intending it, Longarm found himself riding a familiar trail, and in a matter of miles he came to the tar-paper shack where the Thomas family lived.

Calvin was the first to spot him riding into the yard. The boy was busy picking pole beans off a row that was climbing the remains of an old fence. The boy dropped his basket and turned to run toward the house shouting, "Ma, Ma, that man is back. Come quick, Ma."

Mae Thomas had appeared in the doorway by the time Longarm reached the house. She was wearing the same shapeless dress and again had the baby sucking at her breast. She broke into a smile when she saw him.

"Mr. Ankrum. Welcome."

"May I step down, ma'am?" he asked, tipping his hat to the lady.

"Please do." She motioned to the doorway. "Please come in and rest yourself, sir. You will always be welcome here. I want you to know that. Can I fix you something? We have no coffee left, but I make a fine cup of sassafras tea. Would you like some? And perhaps a slab of fried meat off that beautiful steer you brought the other day?"

Longarm dismounted. Calvin darted forward to take the mare's reins and lead the horse away.

"I'm not hungry, ma'am, but I would enjoy some o' your tea that you say is s'good," he said, mounting the step to the porch.

"I have some already hot on the stove, Mr. Ankrum. Come inside, please."

He entered the now familiar cabin and again hung his Stetson on the empty peg beside the door.

Calvin's younger brother—for some reason Longarm could never seem to remember the child's name—was seated at the table, studying his ABCs. He peeped over the top of his slate to stare at Longarm.

Mae Thomas lowered baby Elizabeth to waist level, her distended nipple popping out of the child's mouth when she did so. She carefully laid the baby into her basket and tucked her tit back inside her dress. Then she buttoned the front of her dress before turning to the stove.

A pan of aromatic liquid simmered there. Longarm smiled. It had been a long time since he had had any sassafras tea. The scent of it now brought back memories from his childhood.

Mae fetched a mug from a shelf by the stove and ladled it full of the pale, reddish-gold tea. She placed the mug and a comb of wild honey onto the table along with a horn spoon.

"Use as much of that honey as you want, Mr. Ankrum. Calvin collects it for me. It is one of the things we have aplenty of." She smiled and some of the woman's drab plainness was overcome by the beauty of her smile. "Honey thanks to Calvin and now beef thanks to you, Mr. Ankrum. Our whole family thanks you for that. May I ask you something, Mr. Ankrum?"

"Of course. Ask anything. I won't mind," he said.

"Your visit today, Mr. Ankrum. What is it brings you to us today?"

"Why, I . . . I don't actually know. I was just out ridin'

and next thing I knew I was here at your doorstep." He smiled. "I s'pose I was really just wantin' to see someone normal and kind, someone nice that is. Up there in Salt Spring what I see is . . ."

"Sin," she finished for him.

"Yes. That's it, I reckon. Up there I'm surrounded by sin, but you are what folks are s'posed to be."

"Sodom and Gomorrah," Mae Thomas said. "I told you. That place is Sodom and Gomorrah rolled together."

"Yes, ma'am. I think you're right 'bout that." He scraped some honey from the comb and dissolved it into the sassafras tea, then tasted the tea. "This surely is good, ma'am. 'Tis just fine."

Chapter 39

It was late afternoon before Longarm's meanderings brought him back to Salt Springs—or Sodom and Gomorrah if one preferred—and the KW.

He got the mare settled into her stall with fresh water and hay, then went inside for a light supper. Afterward he hit the gaming tables in the casino but played poorly there, distracted by thoughts of Gomez, of the Thomas family and, mostly, of the robbery gang that was operating so successfully in the vicinity.

It had not escaped his attention that the KW had asked to be paid just before the robbers hit him for the money belt and nearly a thousand dollars of the government's gold. Coincidence? That was, of course, possible. But unlikely.

At the very least, he thought, the robbers got their information from the KW. From the girls. Or from someone at the hotel. That seemed clear enough. Innocent exchanges of conversation just could not account for the information the robbers had about him. They even knew about the derringer he carried.

It seemed possible that a robber would think to look for a money belt on the person of a man traveling away from home, but there was no innocent explanation for them knowing about the derringer too. That was beyond the scope of simple guesswork. Would most men carry both a belly gun *and* a derringer? Not likely. One or the other, sure. But not both. Longarm—or in this case Henry Ankrum—carried both. And both were taken by the robbers, both were known to them.

They had known everything he wore inside or under his clothing.

The pretty ladies of the KW had had ample opportunity to see him strip himself naked. They knew about all of it, even including the little derringer.

His question now was who among them was involved with the robbers.

And who the hell were those robbers anyway?

What he needed, Longarm thought, was some way to predict where and when the robbers would show up again.

Then he smiled and reached for the glass of rye that had been sitting in front of him, untouched, for almost a half hour.

He tossed back the excellent whiskey and tossed his cards in as well.

"You're out for this hand, Ankrum?" the gentleman to his left asked.

"I'm out for this evening, John."

Longarm scooped up what remained of his coins, judging that this evening he was down twenty dollars or more, and pushed back away from the table. "It's been a pleasure, gents," he said as he rose.

"No!" a player across the table from him barked. The man stood and came around beside Longarm. "You ain't taking all that out of the game, mister."

"What the hell are you talkin' about?" Longarm said. "All I'm taking out of play is my own stake. I ain't touched anything that belongs to you."

"Once it's on the table, it stays there until it's been played," the belligerent gent said. "That's the rule."

"Maybe where you come from it is, but not where I'm from. An' I don't figure t'play it that way. Now, leave me be so's I can go up to my room."

The man, who wore a swallowtail coat and a tied-down .45, squared off facing Longarm. He backed up a pace and slipped the thong off his Remington.

"I said, mister, you aren't taking that money out of the game. If you want to leave, go right ahead. But you'll leave what's left of your stake in the next pot."

Like hell I will, Longarm thought.

Chapter 40

"Like hell I will," Longarm declared in a loud, firm voice.

"For God's sake, Tony, sit down and shut up," the man sitting next to the unhappy poker player said, tugging at Tony's sleeve. "You're going to get somebody killed here. Maybe me. I would regret the hell out of that."

"I won't shut up. That bastard there can't be allowed to take money off the table like that."

"It's his money, Tony. Leave it be."

"It's my money, Tony," Longarm said, "and I'll do with it whatever I like, whenever I like."

"No, damn you. You've had your chance to do the right thing. Now I'm calling you out over it," Tony snarled. "Something you should know, mister. I'm fast with a gun. I've killed three men down home in Nueces County, Texas. They all crossed me. Now they're dead."

"All right," Longarm said. "You're hell on wheels with a six-gun. That don't give you the right to tell me what to do with my own money, so shut the fuck up."

"Let it go, Tony," his friend said. "Just . . . let it go for a change." To Longarm the friend said, "Tony's a good man. A good friend. But you got to understand, mister, he blows hot sometimes. And he's serious about this. He'll really do it. He'll really kill you unless you change your mind now."

"No," Longarm said calmly, "Tony may *try* to kill me, but there's others have tried that an' I'm still standing." He grinned at the man who wanted to kill him. "If it's all that important to you, mister, cut loose your wolf an' we'll see who's standing when the smoke clears."

Tony began to look worried. His brow furrowed, and he licked lips that were suddenly dry.

But the stupid son of a bitch had made his challenge and followed it with a brag. If he backed water now, he would be branded a coward. By himself, probably, not by anyone else. Others, including his friends, would not give a fat crap if Tony failed to draw, but a man like him would not understand that simple fact. He would think the world really cared what he said or did. Stupid bastard.

Longarm was hoping that Tony would take his friend's advice to shut up and sit down. They could all get back to drinking and playing cards, and Custis Long could go up to his room—alone tonight, thank you—and go to bed.

That was Longarm's hope.

It was not really his expectation.

And unfortunately, expectation overcame hope.

Dumb Tony clawed the Remington out of his holster.

The man was not nearly as fast as he thought himself to be.

Longarm palmed his Colt and shot Tony twice before Tony's Remington ever came level.

Chapter 41

"Wait right there. You just wait right there, mister," Tony's friend said. "We got to . . . we got to take care of my buddy. We can't let him die."

Longarm really did not much care either way. He walked over to the bar and ordered a rye whiskey.

A tall, thick-bodied woman with orange hair and the beginnings of a mustache came rushing into the casino.

"What happened?" she shouted. "Is someone shooting off guns in here?"

Spotting the group of people who had gathered around Tony, she galloped in that direction, still shouting questions to no one in particular.

The men, including Tony's friend, paid her little attention, but the girls in the kimonos all stepped back and gave the big woman room.

Kay Wallace, Longarm guessed. In the flesh. Quite a lot of flesh. As tall as she was, Longarm guessed she would be approaching three hundred pounds. If you could find a scale that would handle her. A livestock scale, maybe. Something normally used to weigh cattle.

He could see her talking with one of the men in the crowd. That fellow helpfully looked in Longarm's direction and pointed. The big woman began churning her way across the room like a paddle wheeler at full steam.

"You," she said, making the word sound like an accusation. "You killed that man."

"No, I didn't," Longarm calmly told her.

"Of course you did. Everyone says so."

"And I've got a couple things to say to that," Longarm told her. "First off, the man ain't dead. Yet. Dying, maybe, but that ain't quite decided yet. Second, if he does die, it's his own stupidity as killed him. A man his age oughta know better than to drag iron on a stranger without the least idea of how that stranger is apt to respond. Fact is, he drew on me. I had no choice. I'm sure your people will tell you that too."

"So you say," Kay Wallace said.

Longarm nodded. "That's right. So I say."

"You don't seem very upset by it," the woman said.

"Lady, if you want to see a man be upset, talk to him layin' on the floor over there. Me, I'm still standing upright. I got no reason to be upset."

"You may have just killed a man," she said.

"That's right, but if I did, he deserved it. Don't forget, he's the one drew on me. I didn't ask for that fight. I didn't want it. The dumb son of a bitch pushed it on me, and once his hand grabbed the butt of that pistol, it was either him or me. Better him than me, I say," Longarm told her.

"You have no regrets?" she asked.

"I regret that he chose to draw, but that's as far as my regret goes. What happened was up to him." Longarm reached for a cheroot, lighted it, then took a swallow of his rye. "Lady," he said, "you serve mighty good rye whiskey here."

"I'm pleased that you like it, Mr. . . . ?"

"Ankrum," he said. "Henry Ankrum, from Denver."

"My girls speak highly of you, Mr. Ankrum."

"That's nice of them," Longarm said. "I'm guessing you would be Mrs. Wallace?"

"Miss Wallace," she said, emphasizing the "Miss."

"Pleasure," Longarm told her.

"You will understand, I hope, that I must ask you to move along from my hotel," she said.

"I haven't finished my business here," Longarm said.

"You have as far as the KW is concerned," the big woman told him.

Longarm sighed. "Can I come back in to drink and play cards?"

Miss Wallace nodded. "You may."

"All right then." Longarm touched the brim of his Stetson to her and said, "I'll get my things an' move along." He smiled. "With regrets. You keep a mighty friendly establishment, an' I'll miss some o' the, shall we say, fringe benefits."

Kay Wallace tipped her head back and roared with laughter. "A lovely way to put it," she gasped when she was done laughing.

"Then if you will excuse me, ma'am, I have some packin' to do."

Chapter 42

Longarm had no idea where he was supposed to go next. He
needed shelter, that was clear enough, but the KW was the
only hotel in Salt Springs.

Still, sitting on the front porch moping about it was not
apt to find him anything. He carried his carpetbag out back
to the little barn and collected the dapple gray mare. He
saddled the horse and strapped his bag behind the cantle,
then led her back to the livery where she belonged.

The hostler met him in the alley of the big barn. "Turning her in, are you?"

"No, I want t'keep the use of your horse for a spell, but
I got myself thrown out o' the damn hotel. Got to find some
place to put the mare and a place now to put myself too."

The hostler grinned. "Thrown outa the KW? Mister, that
ain't an easy thing for a man to do. How'd you manage it?"

Longarm told him. Aside from the fact that he favored
the truth unless there was damned good reason to shade it,
Longarm knew that in a burg as small as this one, the hostler would hear the details within an hour or so anyway, so
it would serve no purpose to lie.

"Killed the man, did you?" the gent asked.

Longarm shrugged. "Can't say for sure either way. When

I left, he was laying there hurting, but he was still alive.
Dunno what might've happened to him since. Does it make
a difference?"

"Not to me it don't, but our deputy might come arrest
you if the fella does die. You should know that I won't hide
you from him. The man's name is Ricardo Gomez, and he
can't be bought nor turned aside once he gets onto somebody
for some reason."

"That's good to know," Longarm said. "Look, I got to
stay someplace tonight. Can I burrow in your loft up there?
I know not to smoke amid all that hay, and if I have to take
a piss I'll come down here to do it."

"I'd have to charge you for it," the hostler said.

"How much?"

"Fifty cents?"

The way he said it led Longarm to believe that he could
be talked down to a quarter, but fifty cents seemed fair
enough considering that there was no actual hotel he could
go to instead. More than likely one or two of the houses in
town would offer rooms to boarders, but Longarm did not
know which. And it was getting late in the day.

"Done," he said. "Add it to what I owe you for using your
horse, an' I'll give you cash money to cover it all."

"You just rented yourself a loft, mister."

Longarm yawned and smiled. He unsaddled the mare
and deposited the tack inside the crowded tack room, then
tossed his carpetbag into a corner there as well rather than
bother carrying the bag up the ladder to the hayloft.

The tack room smelled of oiled leather—a scent Longarm found particularly appealing, almost as good as the
warm odors of the horses themselves.

"G'night," he said, then mounted the ladder to the loft.

Chapter 43

Longarm woke to the sounds of the hostler feeding his animals. The man grain-fed first, then climbed the ladder to the loft and used a pitchfork to toss hay down.

"Good morning," he said cheerfully. "You might want to know that your opponent in that gunfight last night has survived, no thanks to you. He claims you drawed first, so the deputy will be coming over this morning for a visit. Another thing you should know is that if you want to run, you aren't going to do it on one of my horses. I won't let you."

"Oh, I ain't running nowhere," Longarm said, rubbing sleep out of his eyes and hay off his britches. "You say Gomez is coming?"

"He's on his way here already, or so I hear."

Longarm nodded. "That's fine. There's plenty of witnesses to what happened. I ain't worried. Can I help you with anything until he gets here?"

"No thanks. I got it under control."

"In that case I need to find some place to take a shit an' wash up. Then I think I'll go looking for some breakfast." He grinned. "Unless the deputy sheriff has other ideas about that."

"I'll tell him where you've got to. And by the bye, there's

an outhouse behind the mercantile. Likely you can wash up at the barber's. And the café yonder puts out a passable meal cheaper than the hotel does."

"Thanks," Longarm said as he climbed down the ladder to the ground. The mare was busy eating, so he left her alone and went in search of the necessities to start a new day.

Forty-five minutes later he was sitting at the counter in the town's lone café, working on a plate of eggs and pork sausage. He had just broken a biscuit in two and was using it to sop up some egg yolk when Gomez came in.

Spotting Longarm there, the deputy sheriff put his hand on the butt of his revolver and made sure to approach Longarm from behind. "No sudden moves, Ankrum," he said.

"None planned, Deputy," Longarm said, peering back over his shoulder. "You can see I'm not interested in going anywhere, but I would like t'finish my breakfast and then have a private talk with you."

"All right," Gomez told him, "but no funny stuff here."

"No need," Longarm said. "Will you join me for some coffee while you're waiting?"

"Aye, I could do that." Gomez took the stool next to Longarm and motioned to the counterman for a cup.

Longarm finished eating and paid for his meal and for Gomez's coffee, then motioned for the deputy to join him outside.

"Where can we talk in private?" he asked when Gomez came outside.

The deputy raised an eyebrow but said, "If you really want to be all that private, we can go back to my place. It isn't far."

"Yeah, let's do that," Longarm said.

Once they reached Gomez's house, they went inside. Gomez said something in Spanish to a woman there, presumably his wife. She quickly disappeared.

The room Gomez took Longarm to was almost bare, except for a crudely made couch and two chairs. The only

decoration on the walls was a colorful serape hanging above
a beehive fireplace. The walls themselves were plastered
adobe. The floor was slate.

"Sit down," Gomez said. "No one will bother us here.
Now then, why the secrecy?"

Longarm pulled out his wallet and opened it, displaying
the badge there.

"My name isn't Ankrum, Deputy. It's Long, Custis
Long."

Gomez's jaw dropped. "The one they call Longarm?" he
asked.

Longarm nodded. "One an' the same."

He went on to explain the reason for the subterfuge and
added, "You don't have to take my word about the shooting,
though. There were plenty of witnesses. I ain't worried about
that. But I am interested in this gang of robbers that's working down here."

He told the deputy about his own experience with them
and said, "I know they been tolling you off in other directions so's they'd be free to pull their robberies. That's why
I think I may be able to help."

"I could use some help," Gomez said. "That is obvious."

"For one thing," Longarm said, "I think they're getting
their information from the girls over at the KW."

He went on to explain about pretty Louise and the way
he was turning the screws on her.

"I'm hoping the girl will roll over an' tell us something.
But I ain't counting on it. Maybe she will; maybe she won't.
Remains to be seen. In the meantime, well, my money is
still on the KW and the girls there. Maybe the madam too.
We'll just have to see. I'm hoping you and me can work
together on this, Gomez. I figure the next time you're called
out somewhere, you should let me know.

"I don't want to be seen to be in league with you. This
morning is all right since you're supposed to be grilling me
about that shooting. But we can't be seen to be hobnobbing

together or folks will start to wonder. Better if I keep my distance and we figure some other way for you to tell me if you been called away. If you are . . . when you are . . . I'll watch to see who goes in the other direction."

Gomez nodded. And smiled. "I know just the way we can do it," he said. "Do you mind staying there at the livery?"

"Not if it will help us to catch these sons o' bitches, I don't," Longarm assured him.

"All right, then here's what we will do . . ."

Chapter 44

Longarm picked out a rocking chair in front of the mercantile and parked his butt in it. When the owner of the store came out to talk, Longarm said, "Gomez said he intends to verify my story, see if the witnesses confirm it, which they will. I'm sure o' that. He said I should stay in town an' stay outa trouble until he decides will he arrest me or not."

"The way I heard it, the other fella drew first," the storekeeper said. The man sighed. "I wish I'd've been there to see it. We get some excitement in town for the first time in months, and I'm stuck here working on my books."

"Would it make you feel any better if I was to set here an' shoot some citizen for you?" Longarm asked.

The storekeeper gaped in alarm for a moment. He did not relax until Longarm assured him, "Man, I was just funning you."

"Whew! You had me going for a minute there. I thought you were serious about that."

"No, sir. Well, not unless some of the wounded gent's friends decide to pick up where he left off an' come shoot me their own selves," Longarm said with a laugh.

The storekeeper crossed himself and said, "Heaven

forbid," then crossed himself again. "Is there anything I can, uh, get you, mister?"

"No, but thank you for offerin'," Longarm said.

The man went back inside his store and Longarm stretched his legs out and rocked a little.

For the rest of the day the only excitement was when a cow and her calf wandered into the street in front of the store. The barber organized a troop of half a dozen boys who picked up clods of dirt and small stones to chuck at the cow.

The boys seemed to be having so much fun at the task that Longarm was half-convinced they had chased the cow into town themselves so they could have the pleasure of chasing her out again.

Stagecoaches passed through during the day, one eastbound and two westbound.

By rights, Longarm knew, he should have been on one of them. He should be on his way back to Denver now that he knew Ricardo Gomez was not in cahoots with the robbery gang.

But, dammit, he wanted to see those people behind bars.

He ate a light lunch at the café, then went back to his station outside the mercantile. That was where he had told Gomez he would be, and he damn well intended to be available when the deputy sent word for him.

Chapter 45

Three days later, on Sunday, the mercantile and most all of the few businesses in Salt Springs were closed. Except for the hotel, of course, with its casino and fancy whores. The rest of the town might be prayerful, but not the KW.

Longarm returned to his now familiar rocking chair at the front of the general store. He put his feet up and lighted a cheroot, one of the few he had left.

"Hey, mister. You know that store is closed, don't you? It's Sunday," a kid wearing high-water britches and an ill-fitting suitcoat called from the street.

"Thank you, but I know that already," Longarm told him.

The boy lingered, dragging the toe of his right shoe in the dirt and swinging his foot back and forth. He circled in a little closer, then closer still, until he was standing by the front step only a few feet away from Longarm.

"Did you really shoot that Anthony Birdwell?" the boy asked.

Longarm paused, then said, "Was that his name? I didn't know."

"Yes, sir, that was his name and I hear tell his pap is coming to town today with his shotgun. He says he's going to do for you what you did for his boy," the kid said, sounding more pleased about the prospect than worried. But after all . . . a real gunfight? Right out where he could see it happen? That seemed a splendid possibility to a boy of his age, which Longarm guessed to be somewhere around eleven or twelve.

Longarm touched the brim of his Stetson and gave the boy a nod. "Thanks for the warning, son."

"That old Birdwell, they say he's mean," the boy warned.

"What's he look like?" Longarm asked.

"Old," the kid said. "He's real old." Which Longarm took to mean Birdwell was somewhere north of thirty but still standing upright.

"I'll watch out for him then," Longarm said.

"Are you going to kill him?" the boy asked.

"I hope not," Longarm told him.

"If you do shoot him, can I watch?"

"Now, I am not going to shoot a man dead just so you can have some Sunday afternoon entertainment. But I tell you what. You go across the street there and pick you out a good place to set. Then you keep your eyes open, and if you see Mr. Birdwell coming, you give me a signal," Longarm said.

"Really? I can do that?" the boy said, his excitement rising at this chance to be a participant, however minor, in the sort of gunfight he had only read about until now.

Longarm nodded. "You know what he looks like, so if you see him this afternoon just give me a wave. All right?"

"Yes, sir!" The kid turned and scampered across the street to his assigned post. Longarm could see his head turning as if on a swivel as he looked up and down the street, quite probably hoping the senior Birdwell would be coming, shotgun and all.

Longarm hid a grin, then tipped his hat forward over his eyes. He did not, however, drop off into a doze. That did not seem a very good idea, not if Birdwell really was on his way.

Chapter 46

Birdwell really was old. Longarm guessed him to be at least in his sixties, quite possibly in his seventies or beyond. He had several days' worth of gray beard and wore bib overalls and a straw hat.

Longarm thought he remembered Tony or one of the man's friends mentioning Texas, but he might have gotten that wrong. And for that matter it was not unknown for a young man to leave home and go elsewhere to live and to work.

Regardless of all that, Birdwell was here now.

So was his shotgun.

The gun had a long barrel—only one of them—and looked to be a muzzle-loader. Percussion, though, not flint-lock. It looked like it had been well used over the years. The barrel had a brown patina. Rust? Probably not, Longarm guessed. All in all the gun was more utilitarian than lovely. It was a meat-making tool, nothing more.

Of course it could also turn human flesh into meat, and Longarm had no intention of being on the receiving end of a charge of buckshot out of that barrel.

"Afternoon," he said, tipping his hat as the old man got

close—close enough that it would be damned difficult for Birdwell to miss should he choose to shoot.

"Are you Henry Ankrum?" Birdwell asked. His voice was rasping. He did not sound like a well man.

"I am, sir," Longarm admitted. "Would you be Tony Birdwell's father?"

The old man nodded. "That's right. Come to get justice for my boy."

"I can understand that. How is your son now?"

"Fat lot you care," Birdwell snapped.

"Matter o' fact, sir, I do care. I didn't want to shoot, but he gave me no choice. He drew on me and at that point it was one of us or the other." Longarm shrugged. "I was quicker'n him."

"He's my son," the old man said, "my own flesh."

"Yes, sir, and I'm glad that he's survived. I heard that night that your boy has something of a reputation with a six-gun. I hope this teaches him not to be so free with it, not to go drawing on folks who might not appreciate it."

"You say Tony drew on you first?"

"Yes, sir, but you needn't take my word for it. Ask his friends. I know he had at least one pal there at the card table that evening. I don't know the man's name, but he can tell you the way it went. Tony pushed it. When he drew, well, I had no choice at that point. I had to defend myself, and that's what I done."

Birdwell chewed on his lower lip, uncertainty written plain to see on his weathered face. "I came here to kill you," he said after a long pause.

"Yes, sir. I understand that, given what your son has likely said about the fight. But I have to tell you straight up. If you cock that piece and point it in my direction, I will do the same to you that I done to your boy. I would regret it, but I'd do it. I hope you understand that," Longarm said.

"I came here to kill you, Ankrum, but damned if you

don't sound like an honest man. Did Tony really push you into the fight?"

"Yes, sir, he did," Longarm said.

The old man took in a deep breath and let it out slowly. He looked troubled.

After a moment Birdwell's expression softened. When it did, Longarm could see what he must have looked like when he was a young man.

He had reached his decision and was at peace with it.

Birdwell hefted the shotgun in both hands and draped his thumb over the hammer.

Chapter 47

The old man transferred the long-barreled shotgun to the crook of his left arm, his thumb still draped over the hammer. But then it could be, Longarm realized, that that was simply the way he preferred to carry the gun, ready for a grouse or a quail to leap into flight.

Longarm took in a deep breath. "Mr. Birdwell," he said, "you don't know how close you just came to joining your boy in a sickbed. Or worse than that."

He looked down and saw that his Colt was in his hand, although he did not remember drawing it and had not consciously intended to do so.

Birdwell's eyes widened. "That's . . . No wonder you were quicker on the trigger than Tony was that night."

Longarm stuffed his .45 back into the leather and said, "Sorry about that, sir. I thought . . ."

"I know what you thought, son, but no, I can't find it in my heart to hate you for shooting my boy, nor to fault you for defending your own life. I'm just glad I saw how the stick floats before I tried to kill you." He laughed, a short bark of sound, and said, "All the gladder since it's me would've been laid out in a pine box if I'd tried to shoot you. Anyway, son,

I'm sorry to have jumped to a wrong conclusion and come here with a gun in my hand. I apologize for that."

"No need for apology, sir. I understand completely."

Birdwell hesitated for a moment, then he said, "All right then. Go with God, Mr. Ankrum."

The old man turned and walked resolutely away, his shoulders squared and his head held high, the old shotgun draped over his left arm.

When he had gone, the kid from across the street came running over to stand breathless and grinning in front of Longarm.

"Mister, that was the quickest thing I ever saw. Quicker'n a rattlesnake. Will you show me that draw again, please?"

Longarm shook his head no. He had had about enough of guns and problems for one day. Now he just hoped he did not get any messages from Ricardo Gomez today.

Chapter 48

The message came on Tuesday afternoon in the form of a breathless and panting Mexican boy—one of Gomez's sons, Longarm guessed—who ran up onto the porch, leaned over, and whispered, "He has been summoned to a ranch east of town, señor."

"All right, kid, thanks." Longarm reached into his pocket for a coin to give to the kid, but the boy unexpectedly waved it off, which only served to strengthen Longarm's suspicion that he was Gomez's son.

The boy walked away, no longer in such a hurry now that his mission had been accomplished.

Longarm stood and stretched. Then he headed for the livery, where he collected the mare and saddled her.

Gomez had been called away to the east. That suggested—if this was not a legitimate appeal for the deputy to come—that the robbery would take place west of town.

Longarm pulled out his Ingersoll watch and checked the time. An eastbound stagecoach was due in another three hours, but there was a westbound that would be passing through Salt Springs in fifteen minutes or so. That suggested it was the westbound that the gang intended to hit. If, that is, this was another plan to decoy Gomez away. It could be simply that someone east of town genuinely needed the deputy's services, having nothing to do with robber gangs or stagecoaches.

"Say, you wouldn't have a shotgun I could borrow for a couple hours, would you?" he asked of the hostler who was busy cleaning and oiling the leather trappings of his trade.

"Going to bring down some of our quail, are you?" the man said. "I got a decent old gun in there. It's probably dusty, but there's no rust on it and it's sound. Got no birdshot for it, though. You'll have to buy that for yourself."

"Thanks. I'll bring it back in good shape."

"It's in the tack room there. Right next to the desk." The hostler nodded and went back to his work.

Longarm entered the tack room and found the double-barreled scattergun leaning in a corner beside the desk.

The hostler was right. The gun was dusty but otherwise clean and oiled.

Longarm pushed the lever to break the action. Both barrels were loaded. He pulled the shells—they were goose shot—and set them on the desk, then went out to the mare and stepped onto her, the shotgun in hand.

He rode down to the mercantile and bought a box of buckshot to fit the twelve-gauge. He loaded both barrels with buck and dropped four more shells into a pocket. The rest of his shot shells he deposited in the saddlebags riding behind the cantle of the mare's saddle. If six were not enough to do the job, then he was probably in more trouble than a whole box full of shells could get him out of.

He reined the mare west out of town. He rode at a slow walk down the center of the highway, vigilant to either side of the road. Those hooded sons of bitches might be out there somewhere.

Or not. He would just have to watch and wait and see.

Chapter 49

He found a thicket of live oak about three-quarters of a mile west and pulled into it so that he was more or less hidden from the road. Longarm dismounted and waited there, relaxed and smoking a cheroot until he heard the stagecoach's rattle and crunch as it passed.

The shotgun guard beside the jehu saw him. Longarm gave the fellow a friendly wave.

Taking his time about it, he crushed the cheroot underfoot—it would not do to start a brush fire in this tinderdry country—and stepped back into the saddle.

He rode back onto the highway just as the dust from the coach's passage was settling. He could see the vehicle disappear around a curve about a quarter mile ahead. Just about right, he figured, as he touched the mare lightly with a spur to put her into a fast trot. Longarm wanted to keep pace with the coach but not catch up with it.

Half an hour later he was thinking about giving it up. Perhaps Gomez's call to the east had been a genuine emergency and no robbery was planned for today.

Or perhaps, just perhaps, those three figures who had just appeared in the roadway meant business.

Longarm recognized them. Recognized *what* they were if not who.

Each of the three wore a full-length duster and a floursack hood.

And each was carrying a weapon of some sort. It was too far away for him to see if they were armed with shotguns or rifles today, but it hardly seemed to matter. As close as they were to the stagecoach, either type of firearm would be deadly, including the shotguns.

Longarm could not hear what they were saying, but that did not matter either. He knew the gist of it without having to hear.

He could see the stagecoach guard throw down his own gun even as the jehu was pulling the team to a halt.

Longarm remembered those bastards all to well from his own experience with them.

And he wanted them. He wanted to hang their scalps on the wall. But he was willing to settle for seeing every one of them behind bars.

Longarm threw the steel to the mare, and she jumped into a dead run as he held the reins in one hand and the borrowed shotgun in the other.

Chapter 50

He was fifty yards away, still a little too far to cut down on them with the shotgun. He heard a gunshot from his right, and a swarm of shotgun pellets sizzled past just behind his head.

A fourth robber was standing behind a clump of cactus there.

Longarm had not seen that one, had not suspected the presence of another hooded figure guarding against an assault from behind.

Longarm reined the mare hard right. He charged straight for the hooded figure.

He rose as high as he could get in the stirrups so his muzzle blast would not get the mare too, and then he tripped the front trigger of the double-barrel twelve-gauge.

The gun roared and bucked in his hand. It felt like it damn near broke his wrist.

The gun was not in as good a shape as he had thought. Somehow when he pulled one trigger the first shot dislodged the other hammer too, so both barrels went off almost at the same time.

Bad as the double recoil felt behind the gun, the effect in front of it was devastating.

The duster-covered robber was thrown back off his feet, his entire torso torn and bloody. Even the clump of cactus was shredded.

Longarm hauled the mare to a sliding stop, dropped the shotgun, and grabbed his .45.

The fourth robber had done his job, though. The other three, up beside the stopped coach, were aware of Longarm's menacing presence now. All three of them began firing at him.

Bullets and shotgun pellets flew, several stray pellets striking the mare in the face. She shied away, cutting hard to her right so suddenly it was all Longarm could do to keep his seat.

By the time he had the horse under control, the robbers had disappeared into the brush.

By the time he spurred the mare up beside the stagecoach, he could hear hoofbeats as the robber gang made an escape.

Again Longarm spurred the horse, but the mare had had enough. She sulled, refusing to take up the chase. The mare locked up solid, and no amount of urging would get her to move. Longarm finally had to dismount and lead her forward.

"Are you all right?" he called to the jehu and the shotgun messenger.

"We are. You chased them off, mister. Thanks."

"Shit, I didn't want to chase them. I wanted to put the sons o' bitches in irons," Longarm answered.

There were three passengers, all of whom said they were unharmed.

"I'm sure glad you came along when you did," one well-dressed man said. "I'm carrying money from the sale of a bunch of cattle. They would have cleaned me out."

He would have been the reason for the robbery, Longarm guessed.

"Did you spend some time at the KW?" he asked the fellow.

The man grinned. "Don't we all?" he said.

And that, Longarm thought, explained that.

He checked the mare's injuries. They were slight, but they might well have ruined a good horse. It was too soon to tell about that. He left her where she was and walked back to the cactus patch where he had shot the fourth robber.

The guy was lying right where Longarm had last seen him. His whole chest had been blown away by the double blast of buckshot.

Longarm called to the coach for some help dragging the robber out to the road. While he waited for the guard and two of the passengers, including the grateful fellow who was the object of the robbery, he knelt beside the dead robber and pulled the man's hood off.

Except this man was not a man.

This was a girl. One Longarm recognized from the KW.

"Damn, mister. That's Gwendolyn," the cattleman said. "She spent last night with me."

Longarm grunted and shook his head.

Suspicions confirmed, though. The KW was deeply involved. Pretty much had to be. Although that did not tell him who the man was. He knew there was a man leading the pack. He had heard the voice when he himself was robbed of his money belt.

"Help me pull her out to the road," he said. "An' I'll have to ask you to carry me and the body back to Salt Springs."

"I'll help you get her as far as the road," the stage line employee said, "but that's as far as it goes. We can't go all the way back there. It would throw our schedule all to hell and gone. But maybe she had a horse tied somewhere around here. Or you can wait for our next eastbound to come by. It should be here in another hour or so."

Longarm groused about it, but in the end he had to settle

for waiting for the eastbound. If the dead girl had had a horse, the others must have taken it with them when they fled, and the dapple mare was no longer worth a shit for one man, much less for a rider and a lifeless body. Nor was Long-arm inclined to walk leading the mare all the miles back to town.

The delay did give him plenty of time to think, however.

Chapter 51

"I don't care who or what you say you are, mister, I said I would carry you and that," he hooked a thumb toward the body of the dead robber, "here to town. Well, here we be. Now it's near ten o'clock at night, and I'm not going to leave my route and take you over to wherever the hell the deputy lives. You get off here, and take that with you," the driver of the eastbound coach declared after they made their regular stop in front of the KW.

Longarm grumbled, but there was not much he could do about it. He had no authority over the stagecoach line and could not force the driver to do anything.

He had no idea who the people of Salt Springs used for undertaking services—probably the barber, but that gentleman had long since closed up for the night—and anyway the dead girl belonged to the KW.

Longarm settled his problem by tying the mare to a hitching post and carrying what was left of Gwendolyn up onto the KW's front porch.

He set the corpse down in one of the rocking chairs and went inside.

"Where can I find Miss Wallace?" he asked the petite blonde behind the counter.

"Is it important, Mr. Ankrum? I can take care of almost anything, you know."

"Not this, you can't." He pulled out his wallet and opened it to display his badge. The Ankrum ruse had gone about as far as he could take it. "Tell her Deputy United States Marshal Custis Long wants to see her."

"Dep . . ."

"Deputy United States Marshal," Longarm repeated.

"Like . . ."

"Yeah. Just like him. Now, go tell the lady, will you."

"Yes, sir. Right away, Marshal."

The girl disappeared into the back. She returned a minute later with Kay Wallace practically on her heels.

"Let me see that badge," the big woman demanded.

Longarm showed her his credentials and said, "One of your girls is out front. I'm told her name is Gwendolyn."

"She's late. She was supposed to go on duty at eight this evening," Wallace said.

"She has a good excuse," Longarm said. "She's dead."

"Dead?"

"Very. She and some others tried to hold up the stage this afternoon. Gwendolyn took a double load of buckshot. The others got away. Maybe some of your girls?"

"Certainly not," Kay Wallace said indignantly. "My girls are taught to be young ladies, not ruffians."

"Well, out there's one o' them that ain't gonna ruff nobody no more," Longarm said.

He followed Wallace out onto the porch, where she turned up the wick on one of the coach lamps and inspected dead Gwendolyn. "This is terrible," she said. "I don't allow . . . My girls are well taken care of. They have no need to steal, and they know I won't stand for any pilfering. They know my gentlemen customers can expect to be safe here and properly taken care of. They never . . . they never . . ."

Longarm was not sure who was not supposed to ever do what, but it was obvious that Kay Wallace was genuinely distressed about the robbery, almost as much as she was about Gwendolyn.

"She's yours," Longarm said, "so I reckon you can take care of her one more time, ma'am."

He touched the brim of his Stetson to her and went back down to where he had left the mare.

Rather than fight the horse to get her to walk out properly, he led her back to the livery.

It was only when he was turning into the barn alley there that he remembered the shotgun he had dropped in the brush when he palmed his Colt.

There was no way he was ever going to be able to find that spot again, he was sure. But he suspected he was about to thoroughly piss off one livery hostler. One more thing for the man to put on the government's tab, he supposed.

Chapter 52

"You and me got to talk, Ricky," Longarm said. "Can I buy you a breakfast?"

"I already ate, but I would have a cup of coffee with you while you eat," Gomez said.

Longarm nodded. "Fair enough." He grinned. "This one will be on the expense account, on account of we'll be talking some business."

"If you mean Gwendolyn," Gomez said as they walked to the café, "I already heard about her. Kay Wallace was after me not ten minutes past daybreak this morning, yammering about you being a deputy and did I know it and did I know that you slaughtered one of her girls.

"By now she'll have the body over to Gus Crane's place . . . He's our photographer among other things, queer as a three-dollar bill but a good man with putting makeup on the girls to make them look their prettiest . . . Gus handles what little we need in the way of laying out and burying.

"Kay says Gwendolyn is a mess. All tore up by whatever you did to her. Is she right about that, Long?"

"Call me Longarm if you like. And yes, Miss Wallace is right. The girl's a mess. What happened was that I intended to fire one barrel but both went off. Damn near busted my wrist too. The girl . . . I didn't know she was female at the time, her being all covered up like she was . . . she took both barrels of buckshot right in the chest. Drove a hole practically all the way through her. The buckshot tore her up pretty bad."

"I'm sorry to hear that," Gomez said. "Are you thinking that Kay Wallace is the head of the gang?"

"To tell you the truth, Ricky, I don't know what to think about that. When I brought the girl in last night, she was awful upset by what happened. Either she hadn't known beforehand or she could make a fortune playacting on stage," Longarm said. "And I know for a fact from the time they robbed me that there's at least one man involved, for I heard his voice. He's the only one said anything that time, which suggests it could be that more of Miss Wallace's girls than just Gwendolyn are involved."

"Do you have any idea who the man could be then?" Gomez asked.

Longarm shook his head. "I wish that I did, but I don't know enough about the situation down here, nor the folks, to make any educated guesses about that. I'm hoping you might have some ideas."

"The only idea I have right now," Gomez said as they reached the café, "is that I might cave in and have a second breakfast now that we happen to be here. Whatever they're cooking this morning smells awfully good. Could be crullers. They make the best crullers you've ever put a tooth to, especially when they're hot and fresh."

Gomez pulled the door open and motioned for Longarm to go ahead of him.

Chapter 53

"You son of a *bitch*!"

Longarm ducked under the roundhouse right hand of the hostler. The man was screaming and practically in tears.

"You've ruined her, damn you. Ruined." He tried again to punch Longarm, but Gomez jumped up from his chair and grabbed the hostler around the waist, pulling him back away from Longarm.

"Settle down, Seth, or we'll have to arrest you for assaulting a peace officer," Gomez warned. Not that Seth seemed to be listening. The man kept trying to break free so he could hit Longarm.

"Now, what is this all about, Seth?" Gomez asked.

"Him," the hostler said, pointing at Longarm. "He's gone and ruined my best horse. She won't take her gaits. Won't hardly do anything."

"I can explain," Longarm said.

"I don't want you to explain," the man yelped. "You ruined my best horse. She has bullet holes. In her face, for God's sake. I don't know why you did that, but she's ruined."

"Look, it was in the line of duty that she was injured. I'll give you a voucher for payment. What is she worth? Fifty dollars? Sixty?"

"A hundred," Seth said, no longer struggling quite so much. "She's worth at least a hundred."

"Baloney," Gomez said. "Are we talking about that gray mare? Seth, that horse is old as Methuselah. She can't be worth more than fifty dollars."

"Seventy-five," Seth insisted. "She's worth seventy-five anyway."

Gomez looked at Longarm and raised an eyebrow.

"All right," Longarm said, rubbing his forearm where one of Seth's wild blows had landed. "I'll give you a voucher for seventy-five."

"Plus the day rate when you were using her, plus your use of my loft. Which you aren't welcome to use anymore. I'll thank you to just stay away from me from now on."

"What do you think it all comes to?" Longarm asked.

"A hundred. I'll take a hundred," Seth said. "But you're to get your things out of my barn, and don't come back. And don't think you can use any of my livestock again. Not after what you did to my mare. In her face. Shot in her *face*, for God's sake. She's ruined. Completely ruined now, thanks to you."

Gomez raised an eyebrow.

Longarm shrugged. "I was kicked out of the hotel. Now I'm not even welcome at the livery barn, dammit."

The local deputy laughed. "We can take care of that. You can sleep at my place until we figure this thing out. Soon as we're done here, we'll walk over and get your things and take them to my house. It's no secret now about who you really are, so it can't hurt anything to do that."

"All right," Longarm said, "but we still have to figure out how to handle this road agent problem. Do you have any ideas?"

Gomez sent Seth on his way with the promise of a payment voucher to come later, then said, "No, not really. You?"

Longarm nodded. "Matter o' fact, Ricky, I just might have an idea 'bout that." He laughed. "Miss Wallace might not like it much, but let's see what you think about trampling on some folks' rights so we can maybe get to the bottom of all this."

He glanced around to make sure no one was likely to overhear, then in a low, cautious voice he began talking.

Chapter 54

"Sorry about this bed, Longarm," Gomez said after Longarm dropped his carpetbag at the foot of a bed that was a good six inches too short for his height. "Just curl up like a snail and you'll be all right," the deputy said with good humor.

"I've slept worse," Longarm said. "Look, I don't want to put anybody out of his bed here."

"Oh, it's all right. We do this all the time when cousins come to visit," Gomez told him. "Excuse me for a minute. I'll be right back."

Longarm sat on the side of the bed, but he really did have only a minute or so to wait until Ricardo Gomez returned, this time with his badge displayed on his coat and an extra revolver tucked into his waistband.

"Are you expectin' trouble?" Longarm asked.

"Expecting? No. But it doesn't hurt to be prepared just in case there is some."

"Looks like you're ready," Longarm said. "Reckon we should go over there." He stood, took out his wallet, turned it inside-out, and then tucked it into his breast pocket so that his badge too was on public display.

Together the two deputies walked over to the KW and up onto the front porch.

Once inside, Gomez approached the desk. Redheaded Janice was on duty behind the desk. She frowned when she saw the two deputies approach.

"What . . . um . . . what can I . . . ?"

"Kay Wallace," Gomez said, his voice crisp. "We will see her. Now if you please, young woman."

"Yes, sir. Right away, sir." Janice put aside the ledger she had been looking at and scurried away toward the back of the hotel. Kay Wallace came out to the desk almost immediately, but Janice did not return. Longarm guessed the girl was nervous about the mission that had brought the law in.

"What is it?" Miss Wallace asked.

"We are taking you and every employee here into custody for questioning," Gomez said.

"Some or all of you may be looking at long prison terms," Longarm added. "You might want to see that you don't make things worse for yourselves. I advise you to cooperate. Cooperation will go a long way with whatever judge hears the case."

"Judge? Prison? I don't understand what this is all about."

"If that's true, then you have nothing to fear," Gomez said. "Lie to us and you will feel the wrath of the court, I promise you."

"I still don't understand, but what is it you want from me?" the big woman asked.

"We need to interview you and all your people," Longarm said. "Every one of 'em. So round 'em all up, and let's get this thing under way."

"I have customers here, you know," she said. "I can't leave them unattended."

"You can and you will," Gomez said, "or I will charge you with obstruction of justice."

"Do you really think you can make that stick?" she protested.

"If he can't, then I damn sure will," Longarm put in. "I'd advise you to get all your people together. The casino room is big enough to hold everyone. We'll take them out and talk to them one at a time. Then we'll either turn them loose to go back to their duties here at the hotel or they'll be put in irons and transported for trial."

"You are serious about this, aren't you?" Kay Wallace said. She sounded resigned and perhaps resentful, but Longarm did not think she sounded like she was guilty of anything.

"Dead serious," he assured her.

"Go on into the casino then. I'll have to let everyone know." She hesitated. "*Every*one?"

"Every last soul," Gomez said, "including kitchen staff, housekeepers, girls, everyone."

"Give me a minute then. I will get them for you."

"How is your Spanish?" Gomez asked Longarm while they sat at one of the gaming tables waiting for the room to fill up with KW employees.

"Lousy, why?"

"Perhaps you should let me talk with the kitchen people and the cleaning women then. They are more likely to speak freely in their own language."

"Sounds sensible." He grinned. "That means I get the good-looking ones."

Gomez frowned at that attempt at humor. But then Ricardo Gomez did not like the idea of there being a whorehouse in his hometown, Longarm remembered, and tried to find reasons to close them down. So far he had been unsuccessful about that, but this business with the road agents could be enough for him to shutter the KW's doors for good.

Chapter 55

Longarm was surprised that there were so many employees. He counted forty-two but might have miscounted somewhere along the line. About half were the sporting ladies. The others were support staff of one sort or another, cooks and laundresses and such. They pretty much filled the casino where Kay Wallace had brought them.

He spotted Louise in the crowd and took her by the arm. She resisted having to go with him, but Longarm dragged as much as led her out of the crowded casino and onto the porch.

"Please, sir, no."

"You know what I want to know," he said, figuring that if the girl did know anything, she would think he would know it too and not want to be caught in a lie.

"You won't tell Kenneth?" she whimpered.

"No, I won't."

"Nor tell Miss Wallace about him?"

"Not a word."

"I think . . . I think some of our girls are sneaking off and doing bad things," Louise said.

"What bad things?" Longarm reached for a cheroot,

nipped the twist off with his teeth, and spat out the bit of tobacco.

Louise quickly came up with a match that she struck and held for him to light the cheroot. Trying to get on his good side, he thought. As if he had a good side. He still felt lousy about the way he had treated her, trying to pry information from her.

"Some of them have been going off someplace when they're off duty, but they don't say where they go or what they do there," Louise said.

Longarm grunted. He puffed on his cheroot for a few moments—it was not a top-quality smoke, but it would have to do—before he said, "Are they going with a man too?"

"Oh, no. Miss Wallace wouldn't allow that. Like with my Kenneth. They would get fired if they went off with a man."

"All right," Longarm said. "Who are these girls?"

Louise began to cry. "I don't want . . ."

"You don't have any choice. You either tell me what I need to know, or I have me a nice long talk with Kay Wallace."

"P-p-p-please, sir."

Longarm said nothing. He simply stared at her, his expression stony, his eyes dark.

After a few moments Louise began to speak.

Chapter 56

Longarm tapped on the dining room door. After a moment he heard Gomez call out, "Come in." Longarm stepped inside the dining room, leaving the wide double doors open behind him.

Gomez and a young woman, either Mexican or Indian, were seated at one of the tables. Gomez raised an eyebrow. Longarm took him by the arm and led him away from the table.

"What's up?" the local deputy asked.

"We got some arrests to make," Longarm said.

"Your girl talked?"

Longarm grinned. "Couldn't hardly shut her up once she got to running her mouth."

"What do we know then?" Gomez asked.

"Names. We got the names of five girls who slip away sometimes when they ain't supposed to. You don't have a jail here?"

Gomez shook his head. "When I have a prisoner, I transport him over to Las Cruces."

"You got irons enough for five prisoners at once?" Longarm asked.

"That I do have. They're back at the house, but it will be

easy enough to go get them. Do you really think leg irons are necessary?"

Longarm nodded. "The thing is, once they feel that steel snap closed on their ankles, they're gonna get scared. That an' taking them away from home . . . well, away from the hotel an' everything they're used to . . . that oughta put the fear into 'em. Kinda soften them up for interrogation once we get them over to Las Cruces."

Gomez grunted softly and paused for a moment in thought. Then he said, "I'll go get the irons. Do you know which ones you want?"

"By name. Except for one of 'em. I know her by sight but not the others."

"Ask Kay Wallace to help you identify the ones you want. She should know all of them." Gomez paused again. "I wonder if this will allow me to shut this place down."

"I wouldn't think so," Longarm said. "Not unless you got a judge who'll go along with damn near anything."

"Even if it turns out that I can't close them," Gomez said, "this will put a whupping on Wallace."

Longarm shrugged. "Talk to the judge."

"What about the man? Didn't you say it was definitely a man's voice that you heard when you were robbed?"

"No doubt about it, and I want him, Ricky. I want that son of a bitch bad."

"Yeah, well, in the meantime I'll go get those irons and see if I can scare up a carriage or a wagon to carry them in."

Gomez left, and Longarm went in search of Kay Wallace to help him identify the five girls. Including redheaded Janice. He hated that, but he had been given her name and she would be going to Las Cruces in leg irons too.

Chapter 57

Longarm herded all five kimono-wearing girls in front of him. Gomez returned, carrying the promised irons. He stopped at the casino entrance and waited there.

"Wait a second, Mr. Ankrum. I forgot something," Janice said. Before Longarm had time to respond, the girl turned and headed for the bar. "Just let me get . . ." she said, reaching under the counter.

"Oh, shit," Longarm mumbled as Janice brought out a stubby, sawed-off double-barreled scattergun. "No!" he shouted.

Too late. Janice brought the gun level and tripped one of the triggers. The left barrel belched smoke and flame. And lead shot.

The load of goose shot struck Ricardo Gomez in the left arm and high on his left side, spinning him around and making him drop the leg irons with a loud crash.

By then—but too late—Longarm had his .45 in play.

He did not see that he had much in the way of choice. Before the deadly girl could swing the other barrel in his direction, he triggered a response.

Longarm's slug struck Janice under her right tit. It threw

her back against the shelf of bottles and glassware. She dropped out of sight behind the bar.

Longarm looked at Gomez, who waved him forward. The local man had his revolver out and was covering the other four girls, so Longarm ran past frightened hotel workers and skidded around the end of the bar.

Janice was lying on the floor there, crumpled like a doll that had been tossed aside.

He knelt beside her and took a look at her wound. There was little blood pulsing in the red, dime-sized hole in her flesh, but she was pale and weak. From the placement of the wound he suspected she had been shot in the liver. Perhaps his bullet even nicked her heart. Whatever the damage, she seemed to be bleeding out internally.

Janice would be dead within minutes. He was sure of that.

Biting back an impulse to comfort the girl, he picked her up and laid her on the bar.

"Can you hear me, Janice?" he asked.

She responded with a slight nod of her head.

"I can fix you up, kid. I can take care o' you. But I won't do that unless you tell me who the man is that leads this gang. D'you understand me? I won't do nothing to help you unless you help me first."

"You . . . son . . . of a bitch," she whispered.

"Yeah, but the fact remains," he said. "You gotta tell me who the man is or I won't do anything to fix you up."

She was struggling for breath, and her waxy color already had the pallor of death.

If she could just cling to life long enough to give him the name he wanted . . .

Longarm leaned down close to Janice's lips. "Tell me," he said. "Tell me or I won't fix you up."

Chapter 58

Longarm looked at Gomez. The deputy's left arm was hanging useless at his bloody side, but the man had sand. He had his revolver trained on the other four girls and was fully aware of what was going on. Gomez motioned for Longarm to go ahead.

"What about her?" he asked as Longarm passed by him on the way out.

"Janice, you mean?"

"Is that her name? Yes, the one on the bar there," Gomez said.

"She's dead, Ricky."

"Did you get the name?"

Longarm nodded. "It's Jesse Hood. Do you know where I can find him?"

"Jesse? Jesus. Who would've thought that. Yes, Jesse works at the mercantile. He doesn't own it. He's just a helper there. I never thought . . ." Gomez shook his head. "Damn," he said.

"Where would a man like that get horses for him and the girls?" Longarm asked.

"He races quarter running stock. Makes a good bit of

money off them. At least that's where I always assumed his money came from." Gomez leaned back against the wall.

"Are you gonna be all right?" Longarm asked.

"Sure. Sorry I won't be able to help you with Hood, though."

"Don't even think about it," Longarm said. "Just keep an eye on these prisoners. We'll drive them over to Las Cruces after I come back with this Jesse Hood fellow."

Longarm touched the brim of his Stetson in salute to the gritty deputy, then left the hotel and walked rapidly toward the mercantile, reloading his .45 as he went.

Chapter 59

Longarm walked into the mercantile with his .45 in one hand and his badge in the other. "Jesse Hood," he said. "Where is he?"

"Jesse and me saw Deputy Gomez headed over to the hotel carrying a bunch of leg irons. Jesse turned and ran out the back," the aging proprietor said.

"Is that where he keeps his horses?" Longarm asked.

"Yes. I have a barn and a corral out there. Jesse keeps his stock there."

Longarm brushed past the man and ran out the back of the store. There was no sign of Jesse Hood—Longarm thought he would recognize the man from his previous trips to the store—but four horses were gathered at the hay bunk.

The corral gate had been left open, and it was a wonder the horses had not escaped.

But then perhaps Hood had intended for them to.

Longarm trotted over to the corral and shoved the gate closed, then he looked on the ground for tracks. It appeared someone, presumably Hood, had ridden hard toward the west.

There were a thousand square miles of rough country out there where a man could hide. That did not mean that Longarm intended for Hood to get away from him.

He entered the corral and eyed the available horseflesh. Picking out a rangy blood bay, he grabbed a lead rope off the fence and quickly fashioned it into a makeshift bosal.

Rather than hunt for a saddle and proper bridle, Longarm vaulted onto the back of the bay.

The horse reared. As soon as it had all four feet on the ground again, Longarm nudged it with his heels.

He shoved the gate open and left it that way rather than take the time to close it again.

He put the bay into a brisk trot, guiding it just to the side of the line of hoofprints that he hoped would lead him to Jesse Hood.

Chapter 60

Two hours later he was sorely regretting his lack of a saddle for the stout bay gelding. And he did mean sorely. Sweat and loose horse hair combined to severely chafe his thighs and butt, and he knew he would remain sore for days to come.

That did not stop him from maintaining the chase, however.

The word "chase" did not appear to fit this situation, but chase it was. Longarm knew that Hood's quarter running horses had tremendous speed in a sprint, but they were not suited to a long chase.

He kept the bay at a rocking-chair lope. The gait was easy to ride and did not burn up the animal's stamina the way an all-out run would.

The tracks left behind by the horse Hood was riding showed that he had fled at a dead run. By now his horse should be pretty well played out. That was confirmed by the hoofprints. Those showed that Hood's horse was paddling with its forefeet.

Longarm was sure that sooner or later he would be able to catch up with the man.

That was confirmed when he saw the tracks veer off the roadway and into a thicket of scrub oak.

Longarm had no way to tell if Hood was in there. He would just have to follow the tracks and hope he did not lose them in the jumble of branches and fallen leaves.

He slowed the bay to a walk and reined it toward the scrub oaks.

Almost immediately he got an answer as to whether Jesse Hood was in there.

A lance of flame and smoke erupted from the midst of the tangled branches. Hood's bullet came close enough for Longarm to feel the breeze of its passage.

Longarm dropped off the bay, Colt in hand. He had no idea if the horse would stand ground tied, but he would just have to chance it. He certainly had no time to tie it in place.

Hood fired again, and Longarm smiled. The second shot convinced him that Hood had a shotgun. The range was long for a scattergun. A rifle would have been another matter entirely, but Longarm felt confident he was safe from any normal shot-shell pattern.

He cocked his .45 and braced it against the stunted trunk of a scrub oak.

He took careful aim and sent a round into the brush just to the side of where Hood fired.

"Give yourself up, Hood," Longarm shouted. "You're caught fair an' square, but the charges are only for theft. You'll face jail time, but you ain't killed nobody. You won't hang, so let it go with what it already is. Do you hear me, man? Walk out here with your hands up. I won't hurt you."

He waited only a moment for an answer. It came in the way of another shotgun blast from the inside the screen of scrub oaks.

Longarm fired again and was rewarded with a yelp of pain and fear from Jesse Hood.

"Come out, man, while you still can," Longarm shouted.

"Fuck you, lawman," Hood said back.

The tangle of shrubbery shivered with movement, and Jesse Hood came stumbling out, shotgun in hand.

Hood took aim at Longarm.

It was not a smart move.

Longarm cut the man down with a pair of .45 slugs in his chest.

Hood dropped his shotgun and staggered backward out of sight.

Longarm waited long enough for Hood to bleed to death if he was going to, then followed the robber into the thick brush.

Jesse Hood lay on his side, curled up. Dead.

Longarm stepped around the body, then went in search of the man's horse to carry the corpse back to Salt Springs.

Custis Long opened the door of the stagecoach and reached back to shake Ricardo Gomez's hand.

"You're sure you'll be all right now, Ricky?" he asked.

"Oh, sure. Doc's got me all fixed up." He flapped his left arm, contained now in a sling. "I'll be fine, thanks."

"The girls will be entering guilty pleas," Longarm said. "They'll get reduced sentences because of it." He laughed. "I bet they'll be back to work in no time at all."

"I still want to close that place down," Gomez said.

Longarm grinned. "Oh, I dunno. There's good things you can say about the KW. Believe me. I know." He was thinking about the girls who worked there. The very accommodating girls who worked there.

"Get aboard if you're going, sonny," the jehu called down from the driving box of the stagecoach.

"Take care, Ricky," Longarm said as he swung into the coach.

"You too, Longarm."

"Hold the coach for a minute, Bob. We have another passenger," the stage line agent called.

A young woman, pretty and quite shapely, came trotting out of the line office. The agent helped her into the coach, where she settled on the seat opposite Longarm for the long run up to Santa Fe.

This might, Longarm thought, be a pleasant trip after all.

Watch for

LONGARM AND THE WAR CLOUDS

the 421st novel in the exciting LONGARM
series from Jove

Coming in December!

GIANT-SIZED ADVENTURE FROM AVENGING ANGEL LONGARM.

BY TABOR EVANS

penguin.com/actionwesterns

M456AS0812

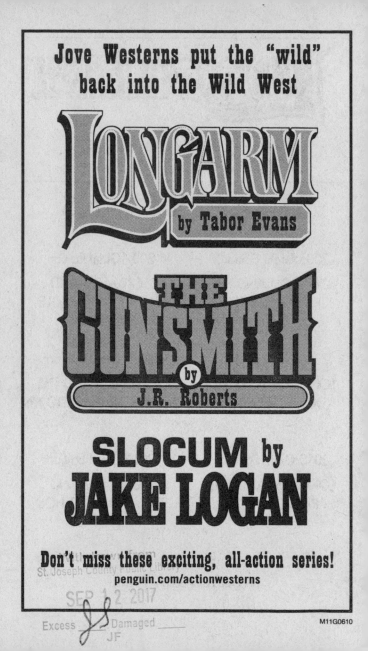